W9-BUE-364

Hiss and Hers

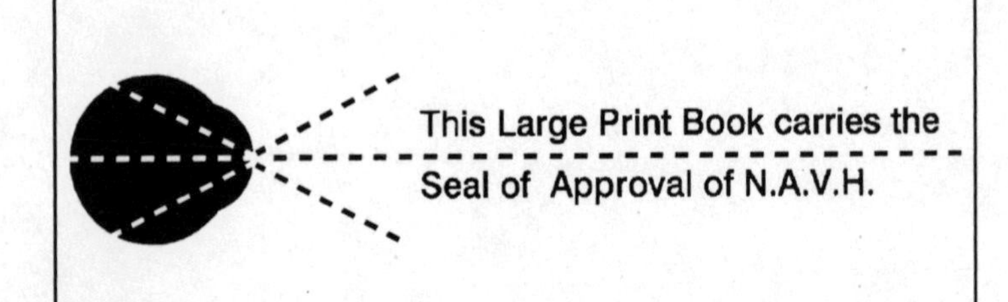
This Large Print Book carries the
Seal of Approval of N.A.V.H.

AN AGATHA RAISIN MYSTERY

Hiss and Hers

M. C. Beaton

THORNDIKE PRESS
A part of Gale, Cengage Learning

Detroit • New York • San Francisco • New Haven, Conn • Waterville, Maine • London

Thorndike Press® Large Print Mystery.
The text of this Large Print edition is unabridged.
Other aspects of the book may vary from the original edition.
Set in 16 pt. Plantin.

LIBRARY OF CONGRESS CATALOGING-IN-PUBLICATION DATA

Beaton, M. C.
Hiss and hers : an Agatha Raisin mystery / by M.C. Beaton. — Large print ed.
p. cm. — (Thorndike Press large print mystery)
ISBN-13: 978-1-4104-5091-3 (hardcover)
ISBN-10: 1-4104-5091-0 (hardcover)
1. Raisin, Agatha (Fictitious character)—Fiction. 2. Women private investigators—England—Cotswold Hills—Fiction. 3. City and town life—England—Fiction. 4. Cotswold Hills (England)—Fiction. 5. Large type books. I. Title.
PR6053.H4535H57 2012
823'.914—dc23 2012032238

Published in 2012 by arrangement with St. Martin's Press, LLC.

Printed in the United States of America
1 2 3 4 5 6 7 16 15 14 13 12

This book is dedicated to
Char and John Sole,
Niki and Michelle, with affection.

Chapter One

Agatha Raisin, private detective, was in the grip of a great obsession. Her friend, the vicar's wife, Mrs. Bloxby, reflected sadly that Agatha, a normally shrewd woman, seemed to lose her wits when she fell in love.

For Agatha had fallen for the village of Carsely's gardener and odd-job man, George Marston. He had worked on her garden until it was into shape and then Agatha, to Mrs. Bloxby's horror, had smashed up her perfectly good bookshelves in order to employ him again doing carpentry.

George Marston, ex-army, was over six feet tall with green eyes and thick blond hair streaked with grey.

But Agatha had fierce competition from the other women in the Cotswold village, and from one very dangerous one in particular. Jessica Fordyce, a leading actress in a long-running hospital drama, had bought a cottage in the village for week-ends. Jessica was in her thirties, petite, with flaming red hair framing a heart-shaped face. And she was witty and amusing. *And* she seemed to need a lot of gardening work done.

Agatha began to grudge the time spent out of the village on detective work. She ran a successful detective agency in Mircester. But she reminded herself that she had moved to the Cotswolds from London and had taken early retirement, although in her early fifties, to enjoy life.

She fretted over her appearance. How could thick glossy brown hair and good legs compete with such as Jessica? Jessica's eyes were large and blue. Agatha's were small and bearlike, looking warily out from a round face.

Things came to a head for Agatha when George rang one evening and said he hoped to take her for lunch the following day to repay the lunch she had previously bought him. "But of course you will be at work as usual," he said.

"I'm free this week-end," said Agatha hopefully.

"Sorry. I'm all booked up. Another time."

I'm sick of work, thought Agatha furiously. I'm going back to being a village lady.

The doorbell rang. Oh, be still my heart! But it was only Mrs. Bloxby.

"Come in," said Agatha grumpily. Mrs. Bloxby noticed that Agatha was wearing full make-up and high heels. She never seemed to relax these days. Agatha was always impeccably dressed and her make-up was a trifle too thick.

"Have a drink," said Agatha. "I could do with one."

"I'll have a sherry."

Bless her, thought Agatha, hobbling into the sitting room. Sherry somehow went with Mrs. Bloxby's quiet eyes and ladylike appearance.

"Why don't you kick off your shoes?" asked Mrs. Bloxby when the drinks were poured. "Your feet seem to be hurting you."

"Oh, all right." Agatha cast one longing look at the window as if hoping to see George's tall figure and then eased her feet out of her shoes and wriggled her toes.

"I've decided to give up," said Agatha.

Relief flooded Mrs. Bloxby's face. "What a good idea. He's really not worth it, you know."

"What are you talking about?"

"What were you talking about?" asked her friend cautiously.

"I've decided to give up work."

"But, why?" wailed the vicar's wife, although she was very sure of the reason.

Agatha avoided her worried gaze.

"Oh, it's such a glorious summer and . . . and . . . well, the truth is I need a break from the detective business."

"But, Mrs. Raisin, although you have an excellent staff, you *are* the detective business." Although friends, they called each other by their second names. It had been an old-fashioned tradition in the now-defunct Ladies Society to which they had once both belonged and somehow they had continued with the tradition.

Mrs. Bloxby wanted to tell her that giving up a successful job to chase after a gardener was ridiculous. But she had come across many addicts in her years of parish work and knew that if you told an addict to do one thing, then the addict would just do the other. And Agatha was in the grip of an addiction as heavy as if George Marston had been a drug.

Agatha called a meeting of her staff on the following morning. Standing around, looking at her anxiously, were Mrs. Freedman, secretary, and detectives Toni Gilmour, young and pretty, Simon Black, also young and with a jester's face, Patrick Mulligan, tall and lugubrious and elderly Phil Marshall with his white hair and gentle face.

"I have decided to take extended leave," said Agatha.

"Why?" asked Phil. "Are you ill?"

"No," said Agatha. "I am in perfect health. I would just like a break."

I wonder who he is, thought Toni. Agatha's been wearing ankle-killing stilettos for the past weeks.

"Let's just go through the cases," said Agatha briskly. "Each of you can take on one of my cases."

"How long do you plan to be away?" asked Phil.

"Oh, until I feel I've had enough time off," said Agatha airily, thinking, until he proposes.

She proceeded to deal briskly, allocating her work. When she left at lunchtime, they waited until they heard her reach the bottom of the stairs and slam the street door. "What's it all about?" asked Patrick.

Phil, who lived in the same village as Agatha, felt he knew the answer. "Agatha's been employing this gardener. I think she's smitten. But so are most of the women in the village. Agatha probably feels she's losing out by being away at work."

"Maybe I could find out something about him to put Agatha off," said Simon. "Toni and I could look into it."

"There's too much work," said Toni sharply. She hadn't forgiven Simon for declaring his love for her and then joining the army, getting engaged to a female sergeant and then ditching his sergeant at the altar.

"I'll ask around," said Phil. "I live in the village, although with the amount of work Agatha's left us, I won't get much chance for free time. We'd all better get to work."

Agatha had found the side mirror on her car had been bent in. She pressed the electronic button to restore it to its proper viewing position, and, as it slid into place, she got a clear reflection of her face. Before the mirror settled back into its correct position and her startled face disappeared from view, she noticed two nasty little lines on her upper lip.

She was seized with a feeling of savage jealousy of the beautiful soap star who had invaded the village. Jessica, unlike Agatha, did not smoke. She went for long healthy walks at week-ends. She did not have to worry about the disintegration of the body that plagued Agatha: the body which seemed determined to have a square shape with saggy bits.

For one clear moment she felt ridiculous.

Chasing after a gardener? What a cliché. But then she thought of George, of his strong body and those beautiful muscled legs, and set her lips in a firm line.

Into battle once more!

She arrived home to find Detective Sergeant Bill Wong waiting for her. He was the product of a Chinese father and a Gloucestershire mother. The result was a pleasant round face with almond-shaped eyes. He was Agatha's first real friend after she had first arrived in the village, lonely and prickly.

"What brings you?" asked Agatha.

"Just a social call. I haven't seen you for a bit."

"Come in. It's a lovely day and we can sit in the garden."

When they were settled over mugs of coffee at the garden table, Bill exclaimed, "I've never seen your garden look more beautiful."

"I have a good gardener."

"Do you know the names of all the flowers?"

"I think I used to, but they've all got Latin names now."

"I thought you'd had a hip replacement," said Bill, looking down at Agatha's high-heeled strapped sandals.

"I don't talk about it."

"You should think about it," said Bill. "Heels that high can't be good for you."

"What's come over you?" snapped Agatha. "You're going on like a nasty husband."

"Just like a caring friend. Who is it this time?"

"What?"

"The heels, the heavy make-up, the tight short skirt."

"Let me point out to you I have always been a well-dressed woman. Talk about something else. How's crime?"

"Nothing major. Usual binge drinkers at week-ends, car theft, few burglaries, no murder for you to get excited about. Why are you home on a working day?"

"I'm taking time off," said Agatha. "It's a lovely summer and I felt the need to relax."

"I see James is back next door." James Lacey was not only Agatha's neighbour but her ex-husband.

"Haven't seen much of him," said Agatha. "How's your love life?"

"Zero at the moment."

The doorbell rang. Agatha leapt up like a rocketing pheasant and ran to the door. Her face fell as she saw one of her other friends, Sir Charles Fraith, on the doorstep. "Oh, it's you," she said. "Bill's in the garden."

Charles's neat figure was dressed in a pale blue shirt and darker blue trousers. As usual, he looked cool, compact and well barbered.

He walked before Agatha into the garden. "Hullo, Bill. How's crime?"

"Not bad. No murders for Agatha. She's just been telling me she's taking time off work."

"Chasing after the gardener?" asked Charles. "They'll be nicknaming you Lady Chatterley soon."

"Wasn't that a gamekeeper?" asked Bill.

"Will you both shut up!" shouted Agatha. "Snakes and bastards, can't I have a break from work without you two jeering at me?"

Charles began to talk about a garden fete that was soon to take place at his mansion, telling funny stories about squabbles among the organisers. Bill listened and laughed, relaxing like a cat in the sun. Agatha was sure her ankles were beginning to swell.

Bill at last said he should go. Charles lingered. He waited until he heard Bill drive off, and then said, "Look, Agatha. There's nothing worse than looking *needy*. Everyone in the village is dressed for the heat. Yet here you are in crippling shoes and a power suit and so much make-up on you look as if you'd wandered out of the Japanese Noh theatre. For heaven's sake, lighten up and be comfortable. You've got good skin and it's buried under a mass of muck. You should go and visit your ex. You were in love with him."

"I don't like being lectured," said Agatha petulantly. "Just go."

As soon as she was on her own, Agatha went up to her bedroom. She selected a tan cotton blouse and shorts. She stripped off and took a long shower and then put on the blouse and shorts and low-heeled leather sandals. She applied a thin layer of tinted moisturising cream to her face and put on pale pink lipstick. She checked her legs in the mirror to make sure she didn't have any hairs on them and then went downstairs.

She sat down at her desk. If she looked on George Marston as a project, a client to be taken over, she might hit on something. Agatha had once been a very successful London publicity agent.

She flicked on her e-mail. The name Fordyce seemed to leap out at her. Where had the cow got her e-mail address from? Jessica was appealing for funds to refloor the village hall.

Agatha phoned Mrs. Bloxby and asked

what it was all about. "Miss Fordyce felt she would like something to do to help the village. The floor really does need repair."

"How did she get my e-mail address?"

"Probably from some former member of the Ladies Society. Do you remember, we all used to have each other's e-mail addresses?"

"Tell her not to worry," said Agatha, her brain working quickly. "I'll pay for the floor and then we'll be able to hold a charity ball. It'll be fun."

"I thought you were going to be resting," said Mrs. Bloxby cautiously.

"A change is as good as a rest," said Agatha sententiously. "We'll make it a really classy event. Full ballroom rig."

It was amazing, thought Mrs. Bloxby, how such a normally hard-nosed detective such as Mrs. Raisin could turn into a romantic teenager when she was in the grip of an obsession.

There was quite a large proportion of the middle-aged to elderly in the village. They became quite excited at the prospect of wearing ball gowns again. A shop in Broadway, a nearby village, which hired out evening suits for men, received a steady flow of orders.

The staff at Agatha's agency received invitations. Toni was thrilled and started to ransack the thrift shops for a suitable gown. Phil Marshall was sure that the whole affair was Agatha's elaborate plan to snare Marston. Young Simon dreamt of wooing Toni. Mrs. Freedman looked gloomily down at her comfortable figure and thought of the gowns she had worn in her youth when she was a slim young lady. Patrick Mulligan was privately determined to invent an illness to get out of the whole thing. He was fond of Agatha and had an uneasy feeling that if he went, he would witness her making an awful fool of herself.

James Lacey, who had found that Agatha seemed to be avoiding him these days, wondered why she was bothering with it all. He could not quite believe that Agatha no longer had any feelings for him. He was really a confirmed bachelor and had felt nothing but relief when the divorce was finalised, and yet a good bit of excitement seemed to have gone out of his life with the absence of Agatha's adoration. He did not listen to gossip and was apt to freeze off anyone who tried to tattle to him and so he had not heard of Agatha's continuing pursuit of her gardener.

George Marston, like himself, was a

retired army man and sometimes dropped in for a drink.

The gardener arrived one evening and settled into an armchair in James's book-lined living room. "Does the leg hurt?" asked James, knowing that George had lost a leg in Afghanistan and wore a prosthetic.

"Sometimes," said George with a sigh. "Bloody women! All this fuss about a ball."

"Oh, that's Agatha for you. Endless energy," said James.

"What happened to your marriage?" asked George curiously. James was tall and rangy with bright blue eyes in a handsome face and he had thick black hair just going grey at the temples.

"Like another drink?" asked James.

"Wouldn't mind," said George, understanding that James had no intention of talking about his marriage to Agatha. "I don't feel like going to this ball but everyone expects me to. What's it all in aid of?"

"The money goes to Save the Children. That's why the price is a bit steep."

"It did seem odd to get an invitation with a price on it," said George.

"Well, that's Agatha for you. Like a pit bull when it comes to fund-raising. In fact, I think she's coming to call. I just saw her through the front window." The doorbell rang.

George got to his feet. "Look, be a good chap and don't say I was here. I'll let myself out the back way."

George hurried off as James went to answer the door. Agatha didn't wait for an invitation. She pushed past James and looked wildly around the living room before swinging round and asking, "Where is he?"

"Who?" asked James.

"George. I saw him come in here."

"He did and he's left," said James. "I looked over the fence at your garden. It looks fine. Do you need any more work right now?"

"No. I mean, yes," said Agatha, looking flustered. "Getting weedy."

"Haven't you got his phone number?"

"Yes."

"So phone him up. Drink?"

"Gin and tonic, lots of ice."

James reflected that Agatha looked much better without those ridiculous heels on.

"How's life?" asked Agatha, taking a big gulp of the drink he handed to her. She wanted to get it finished as soon as possible and go for a walk around the village where she might come across George working in someone's garden. Hadn't she seen him one evening going into the Glossops' house? And it could only be to do work because Harriet was her own age and certainly no oil painting.

"I'm taking a break from writing travel books," said James. "I've been commissioned to write a life of Admiral Nelson of Trafalgar fame."

"I would think," said Agatha cautiously, "that there are a lot of books on Nelson."

"And so there are. Another won't hurt. I'm enjoying it."

"What happened to your television career? You were going to do a programme on expats in Spain?"

"Well, I did, but it hasn't been shown yet. I didn't enjoy it. With the Spanish recession, the high state of the euro, a lot of retired people are finding it hard to make ends meet. And Lord protect me from dreamers. Seemingly perfectly sensible people who have worked hard all their lives suddenly decide to buy a bar in Spain. No previous experience. Not prepared to put in the long hours a Spaniard would. Of course I . . . Are you going?"

"Got to rush. Just remembered something." Agatha darted out the door.

Doing a sort of power walk so that anyone

seeing her would assume she was exercising, Agatha ploughed on through the village under a pale violet evening sky. The air was heavy with the scent of roses. Some people sat out in their front gardens and waved to her. So many new faces, thought Agatha. The recession meant that many people were selling up and richer people were snapping up the cottages and moving in. At least it was not the week-end, so there was no danger of running into Jessica Fordyce.

Carsely village consisted of one main street with a few lanes running off it, like the one in which Agatha lived. There was one general store, one pub, the church, a primary school and, on the outskirts, a council estate. Many of the cottages, like Agatha's, were thatched. But unlike nearby Chipping Campden, there were no cafés, restaurants, antique shops or gift shops so it was free in the summer from tour buses.

It had been said, because of all the incomers, that village life had been destroyed, and yet, there was something in old Cotswold villages that seemed to bind people to them. Agatha herself now felt an outsider when she visited London. Her walk took her towards Jessica's cottage, which was in a terrace of Georgian cottages parallel to the main street. She stopped at the entrance to the terrace. Jessica's little scarlet sports car was parked outside.

As she watched, George Marston came out, shouting farewell. Agatha scurried off, suddenly not wanting to be seen spying on him.

Her heart was heavy, but when she got home, she phoned George. "Hullo, Agatha," he said cheerfully, "you can't want any gardening at this time of the evening."

"I've decided to take some time off work," said Agatha. "Are you free tomorrow?"

"Sorry, booked up all day."

Agatha bit her lip. Then she suddenly thought, what if he does not come to the dance? It would all be for nothing.

"You are coming to the dance?" she said as lightly as she could.

"Of course. And the first dance is yours. Wouldn't think of dancing with anyone else. Got to go to bed. I'm exhausted."

Agatha's rosy dreams came back. She could see them moving together across the dance floor while envious eyes looked on.

Two days of drenching rain brought some much-needed relief to the parched countryside. And then summer returned in refreshed glory. Agatha travelled up to London to buy an evening dress. She spent almost a whole afternoon at Harvey Nichols before deciding on a gold silk gown embroidered with little gold leaves. She bought a pair of high-heeled gold silk evening shoes to go with it.

Agatha was about to get onto the train at Paddington Station in London when she suddenly saw, farther along the platform, George Marston about to board the same train. Agatha had a first-class ticket, but she hurried to see if she could join George in the economy seats.

When she reached his carriage, she was disappointed to see he had a female companion. The seats round George and his friend were full. There was no way she could muscle in. And even if she could, when the ticket collector came around, he was bound to point out she had a first-class ticket and then George would think she was pursuing him.

She sadly retreated to the nearest first-class compartment.

For the first time since her obsession began, Agatha began to feel stupid. She was a rich woman, but all the expense of the ball began to seem mad. It was not as if she could recoup any of the money because it would all go to Save the Children.

When the train finally rolled into Moreton-in-Marsh, she felt clear-headed and somehow lighter. As she was getting into her car, a voice said, "Can you give me a lift?"

She looked up, startled. It was George, those green eyes of his smiling down at her.

"Of course," said Agatha. "Get in."

"My car's in the garage," he explained. "Someone ran me down to the station."

"What took you to London?" asked Agatha. George was formally dressed in a dark suit, striped shirt and tie.

"I went up to join my sister. We had to go to the bank and sort things out. She lives in Oxford. What about you?"

"Buying a gown for the ball."

"Still going ahead, is it?"

Agatha threw him a startled glance. "Of course! Everyone is looking forward to it. Aren't you?"

"Not really my thing."

"But you will be there!"

"Yes, I promised, didn't I?"

"You look tired," said Agatha. "Want to come to my place for a drink?"

"Yes, all right. As a matter of fact, I've been meaning to ask you something."

All of Agatha's obsession came flooding back. Once inside her cottage, she told him to sit in the garden. Her hands trembled a bit as she collected their drinks: beer for George, gin and tonic for herself.

"Now," she said, sitting beside him in the garden, "what do you want to ask me?"

"You're a detective, right? You must have come across many weirdos in your career."

"Quite a number," said Agatha. "Why?"

"How do you recognise a psycho?"

"Do you think you've met one?"

"Maybe."

"Well, there are lots of books on the subject or you could look it up on the Internet," said Agatha. "The trouble is, I think there are different levels. I mean, a captain of industry, say, could be a psycho but it's all channelled into power. He's not going to kill someone. I suppose I would operate on gut instinct. Is someone threatening you?"

"I'm beginning to think I've got an overactive imagination."

Agatha's doorbell rang. She went reluctantly to answer it. "Oh, it's you," she said bleakly to James Lacey.

"I saw George coming in with you," said James. "I'd like a word with him."

"He's in the garden."

Cursing James in her heart, Agatha led him through to the garden. She offered James a drink. He said he would like a whisky and soda. When she returned, James and George were deep in army reminiscences.

At last, James turned to Agatha. "I'm sorry, we must be boring you to death."

"And I must go," said George, getting to his feet.

"I'd better get back to my manuscript," said James.

"I'll run you home," said Agatha to George.

"Don't bother. I'll enjoy the walk. Thanks for the drink." He bent and kissed her on the cheek.

Agatha stood on the step and watched them go. James went into his cottage and George walked down the lane to the corner. As if conscious of Agatha watching him, he turned and waved.

And that was the last time Agatha saw him alive.

CHAPTER TWO

The ball was a sellout. Toni, arriving in her battered old Ford, had to squeeze into a parking place some way from the village hall. Large expensive cars seemed to have taken up most of the parking areas in the village. Simon had offered to escort her and she had turned him down. Now she wished she had accepted his offer, feeling suddenly timid at walking into the hall on her own in all the glory of midnight blue chiffon.

A band up on the small stage was playing an old-fashioned waltz. Toni paused on the threshold, reflecting that it looked like a ball in a society magazine. There was a long bar down one side of the room. She saw Phil Marshall and Mrs. Freedman standing by the bar with Simon and went to join them. "You look very beautiful, my dear," said Mrs. Freedman.

Agatha swung past in the arms of Charles Fraith. Her face was tight with concern. She hadn't seen George for over three days. George had promised her the first dance and yet he hadn't even put in an appearance. She glanced over to where Toni was standing. What it was to be young and beautiful, she thought enviously. Toni's white shoulders rose from folds of blue chiffon and her fair hair was piled on top of her small head. Jessica Fordyce was also standing at the bar, surrounded by men. She was wearing a low-cut black sheath and her glossy red hair shone in the lights.

At the end of the dance, Agatha muttered something to Charles about repairing her make-up, and refused the offer of the next dance with James, but instead she went outside the hall and looked up and down. People were still arriving, laughing and chattering. The county had turned out in force: high voices, out-of-date gowns on some of them, but all at ease in a way that Agatha, always conscious of her low upbringing, could never achieve.

Agatha suddenly decided she simply must find out what had happened to George. She began to run through the village towards his cottage, feeling the straps of her high-heeled sandals beginning to hurt.

George's cottage lay on a little rise above the village. It had been an agricultural worker's cottage at one time, a small ugly redbrick building, unlike the golden Cotswold stone buildings of the rest of the village. Agatha hammered on the door. Nothing but silence.

She wondered whether he might be sitting in his garden, having decided not to attend. Agatha made her way along the path at the side of the house to the garden at the back. It was a mess of weeds and overgrown bushes. Obviously George did not believe in wasting time on his own garden.

Agatha felt a dark lump of disappointment in her gut. She was about to turn away when a bright moon shone down on something sticking out of the compost heap, something metal that glittered.

Moving slowly, Agatha bent down for a closer look and then stood up, her heart beating hard. The metal was part of a prosthetic leg. Maybe he had an old one that for some reason he had dumped in the compost.

She picked up a rake and began to rake away the compost. Another leg was exposed — this time a real one.

Crying and sobbing, she got down on her knees and began to claw away the stinking compost.

Gradually the dead body of George was

revealed, but with a bag tied round his head. Agatha had one mad hope that it might not be George's body but then realised that she did not know anyone else with a prosthetic leg. Agatha felt for a pulse and found none. She wanted to tear off the bag from his head, but a cold voice of commonsense invaded her panic, telling her to leave it to the police. She stood up, cursing that she had left her phone in her evening bag at the hall, and tore off her shoes and began to run, fleeing through the moonlit streets, past the brooding thatch of the cottages, over the cobbles, until she reached the village hall.

The band had just finished playing a number when Agatha Raisin erupted into the hall. She went straight to Bill Wong, who was standing with James. "George Marston has been murdered," she said.

"Show me," said Bill.

"I'll come with you," said James.

"No," said Agatha. "Stay here. Keep them all here. Go on with the raffle. Don't tell anyone."

She hurried off with Bill. "Let's go," said Toni, who had witnessed the exchange. "Something awful's happened. Agatha's as white as a sheet and her dress is ruined." Toni, followed by Phil, Simon and Patrick, hurried after Bill and Agatha.

■ ■ ■ ■

At George's cottage, Bill, who had collected his forensic suit from his car, said, "Agatha, come with me, and just point to where the body is."

Toni, Simon, Patrick and Phil waited anxiously until Agatha rejoined them. Charles came hurrying up. "What's happened?"

"It's George!" wailed Agatha. "I think it's George. He's dead. He's got a bag tied over his head."

Police cars, marked and unmarked, swept up to the cottage. Police began to tape off the area. Inspector Wilkes approached them. "Mrs. Raisin, Wong says you found the body."

"It's in the back garden," said Agatha hoarsely.

"Constable Peterson will take a preliminary statement. Wait there."

Alice Peterson was a pretty young woman with dark curly hair and blue eyes. "Would you like to sit in the car, Mrs. Raisin? You've had a bad shock."

"I'll wait here," said Agatha. "I couldn't see the head. It may not be him."

"I believe Mr. Marston had a false leg.

Did you notice one?"

"Yes, his trouser leg was pulled up," said Agatha. She was wearing scarlet lipstick and it stood out garishly on her white face.

"Just tell me what you know," said Alice.

Agatha swayed slightly and Charles came forward and put an arm around her shoulders. As she told the little she knew, Agatha felt the whole thing was unreal and that the voice issuing from her mouth belonged to someone else.

When she had finished, Charles said, "I went away and got my car. I think you should sit in it, Agatha. Toni, you too. When they get the bag off his head, someone's got to identify him."

They waited in silence.

No other villagers joined them. Amazingly, the news had not reached the village hall, and, through the night air, they could hear the faint sounds of the dance band.

Toni was surprised that Mrs. Bloxby had not come to find out what had happened to her friend. But Mrs. Bloxby, who had organised a raffle for the ball, was holding her post. She thought that Agatha had gone off hunting for George. She had not seen her leave with Bill. She assumed her staff and friends had gone to bring her back.

The night dragged on. At last Wilkes came

out. "We've got the bag off. Someone will need to identify him."

"I'll go," said Agatha, getting out of the car. There were loud protests from her friends.

"No, I've got to see for myself that it is George," she said.

How she was to regret that decision.

In the garden, a tent had been erected over the body. In the unearthly light of the halogen lamps that had been set up, George's swollen and discoloured face was revealed.

"It's George Marston." Agatha gulped and was led back to the car.

"Go home," said Wilkes, who had followed her. "We will call on you in the morning."

The next morning, Mrs. Bloxby switched on the radio as she made her husband's breakfast. She listened to the news, appalled. She went into her husband's study. "Alf, it's ghastly. George Marston has been murdered!"

"When? How?"

"I don't know. I wondered why Mrs. Raisin never came back to the village hall." Mrs. Bloxby regretted the fact that she had thought Agatha had simply been unable to find George and had gone back to her cottage in a massive sulk. "I'll need to go and see if there's anything I can do," she said.

"What about my breakfast?" cried the vicar, but his wife had already left.

The police had put a tape across the road just before Agatha's cottage to keep the press at bay. Mrs. Bloxby, using her status as the vicar's wife, persuaded the police on duty to let her through to the cottage. Toni answered the door, still wearing her ball gown.

"Agatha is in the sitting room, making a statement," whispered Toni. "They should be finished with her shortly."

"Do they know how he died?" asked Mrs. Bloxby.

Toni shook her head. "But Agatha says there is no way he could have fallen into his compost heap and covered himself up or tied that bag round his own head. We'll need to wait ages. If only it was a television show, they'd rush back to the lab and immediately produce the results. Agatha has had to account for all her movements in the last few days."

"I did not see Mr. Marston around the village recently," said Mrs. Bloxby. "The police should ask questions in the village shop. I believe some of the village women were asking for Mr. Marston, saying he had promised to help with odd jobs but had not turned up."

There was a ring at the doorbell. "I wonder who that can be," said Toni, going to answer it.

A smartly dressed middle-aged woman stood on the step, accompanied by Detective Constable Alice Peterson.

"This is Mrs. Ilston, Mr. Marston's sister from Oxford," said Alice. Unlike her brother, Mrs. Ilston was dark-haired and only medium height. Her eyes were swollen with recent crying.

Alice went into the sitting room and emerged shortly, followed by Inspector Wilkes, Bill Wong and a policewoman.

"I wanted to see the man in charge of the case," said Mrs. Ilston. "They told me at headquarters you would be here."

"We'll take you back to headquarters," said Inspector Wilkes soothingly. "I gather two of my detectives broke the sad news to you last night."

"Yes, and I don't understand it!" wailed his sister. "He was always so popular."

They moved off. The door slammed behind them. Agatha dragged herself from the sitting room.

"Thanks, Toni," she said. "You can go home now."

"Are you sure?"

"I'll look after her," said Mrs. Bloxby firmly.

Toni hesitated. She wanted to give Agatha a reassuring hug, but somehow Agatha was not the sort of person one hugged.

"I'll be back in the office tomorrow," said Agatha wearily. "Open a file on George."

Mrs. Bloxby made tea and carried a tray out to the garden. It was a riot of colour: red, white and yellow roses, delphiniums, hollyhocks, pansies and wallflowers, and a large clematis with purple petals that bloomed in the summer instead of the spring. Agatha's cats, Hodge and Boswell, played on the smooth lawn. A few wispy white clouds floated over the blue sky above.

"This is the sort of summer people, when they get old, will remember as happening every year. People forget the rainy days."

Agatha began to cry. "I d-don't w-want to g-get old," she sobbed.

"You're ageless," said Mrs. Bloxby briskly. "Dry your eyes, drink your tea, light one of your rotten cigarettes and start thinking. Someone murdered George Marston."

Agatha meekly did as she was told. "I don't know where to start," she said. "Do you think it has anything to do with his military service?"

"I think perhaps it was too personal a murder for that."

"Someone in the village?"

"Perhaps."

"But why?"

"If you work very hard on this, I will pray you find out."

"Do you believe in God?" asked Agatha.

"Of course."

"Why?"

Mrs. Bloxby put down her teacup, and said gently, "I need to believe in something perfect and unchanging in this imperfect world. Humans are apt to make other humans into gods and being human they let them down. I sometimes think that inside everyone is a desire for a spiritual belief and sometimes it gets twisted. Why else would people worship, say, Hitler or Elvis Presley?"

Agatha laughed, feeling her inner torment ease. "I think you could make a lot of Elvis fans furious with a statement like that."

"You must have had very little sleep," said Mrs. Bloxby. "Go to bed. I will wait down here for a little. Go on!"

Before Agatha climbed into bed, she opened her window and looked down into the garden. Mrs. Bloxby was sitting quietly, her face turned up to the sun.

Agatha left the window open and, despite the warmth of the day, pulled the duvet up to her chin and fell asleep.

After half an hour, Mrs. Bloxby's mobile phone rang. She walked down the garden with it. "Yes?"

"It's me. Your husband. Remember me?" came the vicar's angry voice. "Are you still with that bloody woman? I haven't had my breakfast."

"Put two rashers of bacon and two eggs in the frying pan," said Mrs. Bloxby patiently. "Make coffee. Put two slices of bread in the toaster. I will be home shortly."

Then she rang off and went to resume her seat in the garden. After another half hour, she went upstairs and looked at Agatha, who was sleeping peacefully.

It's safe to leave her now, thought Mrs. Bloxby. When she is stronger, that's when I will tell her that her precious gardener was sleeping with quite a few women in the village.

In her office the next morning, Agatha said, "Until we know exactly how George was killed, I don't really see how we can begin investigations. We'll just get on with the regular work at the moment. I'll take the Callen case. Mr. Callen wants proof of his wife's infidelity. You'd better get your camera stuff and come with me, Phil."

Before she left, she allocated cases to the rest of her staff.

"I really wonder who killed George," said Phil when he and Agatha were parked outside Mrs. Callen's house.

"Like I said, better wait for the autopsy and then we'll have a clearer idea. I'll get Patrick to keep in touch with his old police contacts so we'll know when the results come through," said Agatha. "There's Mrs. Callen, getting in her car. I hope it isn't going to be just another day's shopping."

With Agatha driving, they followed Mrs. Callen at a sedate pace. Unlike previous times, she did not go into the centre of Cirencester but turned off onto the motorway.

"A change at last!" said Agatha.

"Keep back a bit so she doesn't notice us," said Phil. "Of course, I gather he did sleep around a bit."

"Who? Our client, Mr. Callen?"

"No. George Marston. Agatha! You nearly hit that lorry. Pay attention!"

"My George?"

"I'll tell you afterwards," said Phil. "If you

don't keep your wits about you, we'll lose her."

Agatha drove grimly on, her mind in a turmoil. She could understand George falling for the charms of Jessica Fordyce — but who else?

"Name one of the women," barked Agatha.

"Later," pleaded Phil. "Keep your mind on the job."

They followed Mrs. Callen all the way into Oxford. She drove into the car park at the Randolph Hotel. "Drive on and park in Gloucester Green," Phil said. "We don't want her seeing us. Your photo's been in the newspapers and she might recognise you."

The underground car park at Gloucester Green was expensive and they lost valuable time feeding pound coins into the meter. Then they hurried back to the hotel.

"I forgot about being recognised," mourned Agatha. "I should have sent Patrick."

"Wait outside and I'll take a look round," said Phil.

Phil looked in the bar first. Mrs. Callen was seated in a corner with a young man. Could be her son, thought Phil. Does she have a son? Damn! The file's in the car. He ordered a beer and sat down, covertly bringing out a micro camera from his bag.

They were laughing and joking. Mrs. Callen, Phil guessed, was in her late forties and the young man must have been in his twenties. She was a hard-faced woman, heavily made up with a collagen-enhanced mouth. As Phil watched, the young man raised her hand to his lips and kissed it. He shot off a photograph. Then the young man leaned forward and kissed her on the mouth. Bingo! thought Phil. Now if they go up to a room together, we've got her.

Outside, Agatha paced up and down in the sunlight. Over at the Martyrs Memorial, a preacher was waving a copy of the Bible and haranguing an audience of five on their sins.

To her relief, Phil emerged. "I got two good shots of them kissing," he said, "and now they've gone upstairs to a room. We'll need to wait and follow the young man she's with and find out who he is."

"A young man!" exclaimed Agatha bitterly. "Some women have all the luck. It's so hot. There's a shady bit on the other side of the road. We can sit on the steps of the Ashmoleun and wait for them to emerge."

They sat down on the steps of the museum. Buses rolled past on Beaumont Street. Students walked to and fro. Agatha lit a cigarette.

"You'll damage your lungs," said Phil severely.

"Leave me alone," snapped Agatha. "I suppose George was sleeping with Jessica."

"According to village gossip," said Phil. "But that's not always reliable."

"Who else?"

"There were rumours about Mrs. Glossop."

"Can't be!" Agatha felt almost tearful. Mrs. Glossop was her own age but was built like a cottage loaf and wore thick glasses. "Why didn't you tell me?"

"I didn't know it was important to you," said Phil defensively. "You've always said that village gossip is boring. I got them on my little camera and . . ."

"Who?"

"Callen and her fellow, of course. I've got my proper one at the ready. With all the tourists around, they won't notice."

The hot afternoon dragged on. "Here," said Phil, taking a plastic bag out of one of his capacious pockets. "Put your cigarette butts in this. You can be arrested for chucking them on the ground that way."

Agatha picked them up, and then, as she straightened up, Phil said, "Here they are!"

Mrs. Callen and her young man appeared.

He caught her in his arms and kissed her passionately. Phil's camera clicked busily. Then the couple walked into the hotel car park at the side.

"Shall I get the car?" asked Phil.

"Wait," said Agatha. "I've a feeling that young man lives in Oxford. We've got enough for Mr. Callen anyway."

The young man emerged alone from the car park. Agatha and Phil set off in pursuit. They followed his long, rangy strides through the crowds of the Cornmarket and down the High, where he turned in at the gates of St. Botolph's.

Agatha went into the porter's lodge, a crisp twenty-pound note in her hand. "That young man hurrying across the quad," she said. "I thought I recognised him. Who is he?" The note changed hands.

The porter darted from his cubbyhole and looked across the green expanse of the quad. "Oh, that's Mr. Richard Thripp, one of our research fellows."

"Made a mistake," said Agatha. "But thanks all the same."

They returned to the office in Mircester, Agatha to prepare her report and Phil to print up his photos.

But Agatha found Mrs. Janet Ilston,

George's sister, in her office.

"I've been waiting for you, Mrs. Raisin," she said. "I want you to find out who murdered my brother. I looked you up on the Internet."

"I'll do my best," said Agatha. "I'll need to take some notes. Why did your brother say he wished to settle in Carsely? I never asked him."

"After he was injured and went through the rehabilitation process two years ago," said his sister, "he settled in a village in Oxfordshire, Lower Sithby. He started to do odd jobs, gardening, carpentry, things like that. Much as I loved my brother, he was always getting into trouble with women. He had so many affairs and caused a lot of bad feeling. So he moved to Carsely."

Agatha wrote steadily while her mind admonished her sternly — how could you be such a fool? You, who pride yourself on your intuition.

"Do you think," asked Agatha, "that one of the women from Lower Sithby might have followed him to Carsely to kill him?"

"It's possible."

"Do you have the names of any of these women?"

"Just one. Fiona Morton, calls herself Fee, very neurotic. She came to see me in Oxford, crying and threatening revenge and claiming George had taken her virginity."

"How old?"

"Thirty-eight."

"Did you think she was telling the truth?"

"Well, she was very plain and spinster-like. Could be. George vehemently denied the whole thing but that was when he decided to move to the Cotswolds."

Agatha asked several more questions, took down Janet's address and phone number, and then Mrs. Freedman drew up a contract.

"Do your best," urged Janet as she left. "George could be infuriating but no one deserves such a death."

"Are the results of the autopsy through yet?"

"Not yet. They've promised to let me know immediately."

CHAPTER THREE

When Agatha returned to the office, Mrs. Freedman told her that the police had called and she was to report to headquarters.

What now? wondered Agatha.

She waited impatiently at police headquarters until she was ushered into an interview room. Inspector Wilkes entered with Bill Wong. The tape was switched on and the interview began. Agatha was taken through the whole thing again. Wilkes wanted to know what she had done the day of the ball, at the ball, and right up to finding George's body.

Agatha answered as patiently as she could, and then Wilkes said, "That will be all for now, except for the fact that this is a search warrant for your home."

"What! Why?" demanded Agatha furiously.

"George Marston was drugged with Rohypnol, commonly known as the date-rape drug or roofies. He had ingested a massive dose. When he was unconscious, someone put, possibly, three adders in a bag and tied it over his head. The vipers bit his face and so he died of the venom. We are searching for anyone who may have purchased the drug."

"Adders? Snakes?" said Agatha, bewildered. "Where would anyone get them?"

"It's a hot summer and that brings them out but mostly in places like the Malvern Hills."

"But I don't understand," wailed Agatha. "Why so elaborate and vicious?"

"It could be," said Bill in his quiet Gloucestershire accent, "that someone meant to come back when all was quiet and remove the bag. That way it might look as if he had fallen asleep in his garden and had then been attacked by the adders."

"Did you find the adders in the bag?" asked Agatha.

"No, they had probably wriggled out," said Bill. Agatha repressed a shudder as she thought that the snakes might still have been in George's garden when she found the body.

"But do adders just attack like that?" she asked.

"We think that when the bag with them

was forced down over the head, they panicked and struck several times. There were snakebites all over his face," said Bill. "You're looking white. You had better go home."

"That will be all," said Wilkes. "A forensic team is waiting outside your cottage. Let them in to search and wait outside."

Agatha suddenly remembered her last conversation with George. "I forgot!" she said. "George had asked me about how to recognise a psychopath. I told him what I knew and asked him if he had met one and he said, 'Maybe.' Then James Lacey arrived and George eventually left and that was the last I saw of him. Do they know when he died?"

"It's never accurate," said Bill, "but at least twenty-four hours before you found him."

Agatha sat in a chair in her front garden. She still felt numb with shock. Mrs. Bloxby, whom she had phoned on the road home, was sitting with her.

"Did you know George had been tomcatting in the village?" asked Agatha.

"I did hear some gossip," said Mrs. Bloxby cautiously.

"Why didn't you tell me?"

"Because it would have hurt you and I had no proof. For all I knew, it could have been wishful thinking on the part of some of the women."

"What women?"

"It is only rumour and gossip, Mrs. Raisin. I can't really . . ."

"Out with it," commanded Agatha brutally. "I'll find out anyway. I heard about Mrs. Glossop."

"Well, if you must. It is rumoured he had affairs with Jessica Fordyce, Miss Hemingway and Mrs. Freemantle."

"Jessica Fordyce I can understand," said Agatha bitterly. "But Joyce Hemingway is a shrivelled-up spinster and Mrs. Freemantle is just, well, ordinary. And isn't there a Mr. Freemantle?"

"He's abroad on business, I believe. He's something in oil. I believe any of these three ladies could plot such a vicious death," said Mrs. Bloxby.

Agatha sat silently for a few minutes, guiltily remembering the strength and madness of her own obsession. And it did now seem like madness. What on earth had happened to her?

At last she said, "George's sister has hired me to investigate. I'd better start off with these three."

"Mrs. Raisin! You can't just go crashing in and demand whether they had been sleeping with Mr. Marston and whether they killed him."

"Watch me," said Agatha.

The only pills in Agatha's cottage turned out to be an old bottle of aspirin, yet the searchers bagged it up and took it away, no doubt in the hope that the innocent-looking aspirin tablets would turn out to be something more sinister.

When the police and Mrs. Bloxby had left, Agatha phoned Toni and told her that she would be working on George's case the following day and would not be in the office.

She slept uneasily that night, tossing and turning in nightmares through which long snakes slithered in and out.

When she awoke the next morning, the sunny dry weather had changed. It was still hot, but sticky and humid with a thin veil of cloud covering the sky.

Agatha washed and dressed, fed her cats, had her usual breakfast of two cigarettes and a cup of strong black coffee, and set out to interview Mrs. Glossop.

Mrs. Glossop's garden glowed with flowers, a mute testament to the gardening skills of George Marston.

Agatha rang the bell. When the small

plump figure of Mrs. Harriet Glossop answered the door, Agatha looked at her curiously. With her curly brown hair going slightly grey, round face and rosy cheeks, Harriet Glossop looked every bit of her fifty years.

"Oh, Agatha," she said cautiously. "What brings you?"

"Mrs. Ilston, George's sister, has asked me to investigate his murder."

Tears welled up in Harriet's faded blue eyes behind her thick glasses. "I can't get over it," she said. "Come in. We'll go through to the back garden. It's too hot to sit in the house."

When they were seated at a garden table, Harriet asked, "How did he die? Do they know?"

Agatha told her, with brutal frankness, which she immediately regretted, because the colour drained from Harriet's face and she clutched on to the table for support.

"Can I get you something? A glass of water?" asked Agatha anxiously.

"I'll be all right in a minute," said Harriet. "So awful! Such a shock. Such a dear man."

"I believe he did your garden," said Agatha.

"Oh, yes, and little jobs around the house,

like changing fuses and tap washers. My husband, Fred, is separated from me, and it was so nice to have a man to rely on."

"Were you close?"

"We were such friends. He said no one could bake cakes like me."

Agatha took the plunge. "Did you have an affair with him?"

Harriet's cheeks were now red with embarrassment. "It was only the one time," she said in a low voice. "I never referred to it again. I was frightened it would scare him away."

"How did it happen?" asked Agatha.

"It was one evening. He said he was tired and he would like to cuddle up to a nice warm woman. I said, 'What about me?' I was only joking but he smiled that lovely smile of his and he said, 'Why not?' "

"The police will no doubt ask you this," said Agatha, "because someone is going to gossip about you sooner or later. What were you doing the day of the ball?"

"I was down at my sister Edie's in Moreton. She was helping to prepare me for the ball. When I was dressed, she drove me up to the village hall and left me there. I was at the ball right until the end." She began to cry, great gulping sobs shaking her body.

"There, now," said Agatha awkwardly. And

feeling like a coward, she added, getting to her feet, "I'll leave you with your grief."

Agatha was annoyed with herself as she walked away. Her detective abilities were slipping. George had been killed at least twenty-four hours before the ball.

Agatha got no reply at Jessica's cottage. A neighbour said she had come down from London just for the ball and had left early the next morning.

Joyce Hemingway lived quite near Jessica, and Agatha found her working in her front garden. Surely George couldn't have an affair with her, was Agatha's first thought. Joyce was tall, thin and flat-chested, dressed in a pair of old jeans and a man's checked shirt. She had an angular face and grey eyes under heavy lids and a mean little mouth.

Joyce rose from a flowerbed she had been weeding and stood up with her hands on her hips. "What does our local snoop want with me?" she demanded.

"I am investigating George's murder on behalf of his sister and . . ." began Agatha, but that was as far as she got.

"Shove off!" shouted Joyce. "I'll speak to the police but not to you."

"Don't you want to find out who murdered George?" demanded Agatha.

"I'd rather rely on the skills of the police than on one silly village woman who fancies herself to be a detective. How George and I used to laugh about you!"

"I don't believe you," said Agatha, her face flaming.

"Oh, yes, he used to tell me how you were pursuing him. 'I wouldn't have anything to do with that one,' he said. 'She'd eat me alive.' "

"Bitch!" howled Agatha, and stumbled off. She walked a little way from Joyce's cottage and leant against a garden wall to compose herself. How awful if George had really said those things about her. She felt quite tearful and very, very silly.

She should have told the police about George's affairs, but somehow had felt she could not. She had not really wanted to believe the gossip. There was still Mrs. Freemantle to visit. Agatha realised that she would at least have to tell Bill Wong. The police had the resources to find out where, say, Mrs. Glossop's husband had been on the night of the murder and also the whereabouts of Mr. Freemantle.

She miserably took out her mobile phone. Agatha had always prided herself on being a clever, intuitive woman. But she had not recognised a philanderer in George.

Bill listened to her, and then said sharply, "I'll be right over to take a statement. This could be important."

Agatha's cleaner, Doris Simpson, was working away when Agatha returned to her cottage to await the arrival of Bill.

"Isn't it awful," said Doris. "I've made you some nice lemonade. It's in the fridge."

"I'm waiting for the police," said Agatha. "Pour us a couple of glasses and we'll take a break in the garden."

Doris settled comfortably into a garden chair after she had served the lemonade. The two cats jumped on Doris's lap and began to purr loudly. Agatha surveyed her cats with a jaundiced eye. She rarely had any sign of affection from the beasts, she thought.

"Why are the police coming?" asked Doris.

"I found out about George's affairs. They'll need to know. Did you know?"

"Heard rumours," said Doris. "Bit of a lad, that one was. But no one deserved a nasty death like that. It's so hot. Your garden needs watering."

"Sod the garden," said Agatha passionately. "Let it rot."

The sunlight glittered on Doris's thick

glasses, hiding her expression. But she said, "I'll send my man round to do it for you. I'd better get back to work." The cats followed her back into the cottage.

Agatha lit a cigarette. It tasted awful. Maybe smoking is giving up me instead of the other way round, she thought, stubbing out the cigarette.

The doorbell rang and she could hear Doris saying, "Agatha's in the garden."

Bill Wong came into the garden, followed by Alice Peterson. They sat down at the table. Bill said, "Have you been holding back information?"

"I only just found out about it," lied Agatha.

Bill put a tape recorder on the table and switched it on while Alice produced her notebook.

Agatha described what she knew about George's affairs, averting her eyes from Bill's sympathetic expression. Had her obsession been so obvious?

"Before George Marston moved here," said Agatha, "he lived in Lower Sithby in Oxfordshire. A woman called Fiona Morton was involved with him. Apart from the others, that's all I know. Mrs. Ilston, George's sister, has asked me to investigate."

Bill switched off the tape recorder. "I'll

get this typed up and I want you to drop into headquarters this afternoon and sign it."

"Okay," said Agatha bleakly. "Like some lemonade?"

"No, thanks," said Bill. "I'd better get back with this. A word of warning. This was a particularly nasty murder. Yes, people can collect adders, but someone would really have to know what they were doing to collect three of them. It's a hot summer and that's what brings them out."

After Bill and Alice had left, Agatha wriggled her bare toes in her sandals and wondered what to do next. The clammy heat of the day was making her feel lethargic. But she felt the only way she could restore her battered self-esteem was to solve the murder. She still felt humiliated by Joyce Hemingway's attack on her. She gave herself a mental shake. She was never going to solve anything sitting in her cottage. Agatha set off to interview Mrs. Freemantle.

Another cottage garden, heavy with the scent of flowers. Agatha rang the bell and waited. She was just about to turn away when Mrs. Freemantle answered the door. She was a small trim woman with a pleasant face and brown hair. But her brown eyes were red with crying.

"Is it about George?" she asked.

"Yes," said Agatha, acidly noticing the plain hairstyle and the fine wrinkles on Mrs. Freemantle's face and wondering why she, Agatha, had wasted so much money on hairdressing and nonsurgical facelifts, not to mention a whole new wardrobe, all to lure George. "His sister has hired me to investigate his murder."

"Come in," said Mrs. Freemantle. "We'll sit in the garden."

She led the way to the back garden. Red rambling roses tumbled in glorious profusion round the back door.

When they were seated, Agatha asked, "Did George give you any clue as to who could hate him so much?"

"No," said Mrs. Freemantle. "It's all so awful. He chatted away about the army, the weather, the garden — things like that." Her voice broke. "He was a lovely man."

"Nonetheless," said Agatha harshly, "it appears he was a philanderer."

"That cannot be true! He was always the perfect gentleman."

"So you were not aware that he was having affairs with women in the village?"

"No!"

"Did he have an affair with you?"

"No, he did not. I am a married woman!"

"He had an affair with at least one married woman. There may be others."

"It never crossed my mind," she said plaintively. "I mean, what one of us could compete with Jessica Fordyce?"

"Did he say he was keen on her?"

"He did say one day that she was very beautiful and he wished he didn't have a metal leg and that he was younger."

"I'll have a word with her when she comes down for the week-end."

Almost timidly, Mrs. Freemantle asked, "Are you *sure* he was having these affairs?"

"I'm afraid so."

"He was so handsome. But he treated me like a dear friend, nothing more."

"Mrs. Freemantle . . ."

"Sarah, please."

"Sarah, then. Here is my card. If you can think of anything at all, let me know. Is your husband away?"

"Yes, he's in charge of a rig up in Aberdeen. It gets rather lonely. That's why I enjoyed George's company so much. It seems so silly now, but I used to make work for him."

Agatha thought bitterly of how she had sabotaged a perfectly good set of bookshelves in order to see more of him.

She said goodbye to Sarah and walked through the stifling heat back to her cottage.

Her friend Sir Charles Fraith was waiting on the doorstep. "Been out sleuthing?"

"Yes," said Agatha. "Come in and I'll tell you all about it."

When she had finished, Charles said, "Poor you."

"Why, 'poor me?' " snapped Agatha.

"All that titivating and all to be upstaged by the village frumps, except for the beautiful Jessica, of course."

"I was not interested in him," said Agatha furiously.

"Oh, pull the other one, sweetheart. I tell you what. I'm bored. Let's drive down to this Lower Sithby and see this Fiona Morton."

"Have to do a detour to Mircester first. I've got to sign a statement. I'll get changed."

"Don't. You look human for the first time in ages."

As they drove off, Agatha glanced at James's cottage. "I think he's away," said Charles. "When I found you were out, I rang his doorbell."

Odd, thought Agatha. Usually James

would have called to see how the murder case was progressing. "I wonder where he's gone?"

"We'll ask him next time we see him. Thank goodness your car's got good air-conditioning."

After Agatha had signed her statement, they drove off towards Oxfordshire.

"I'll need to sleep in it if this heat goes on," said Agatha. "Rats! I forgot to look up Lower Sithby on the map. There's an ordnance survey map of Oxfordshire in the glove compartment. Look up Lower Sithby and guide me there."

Lower Sithby was a small village of grey stone houses nestling round the long curve of an old drove road. "That's a jolly-looking pub," said Charles. "I'm hungry. Let's get a bite to eat and find out where this Fiona lives."

"Can't we just get on with it? I have her address."

"Food first. Never interview on an empty stomach."

The inside of the pub belied the charming exterior. It was dark and shabby. There was a glass case on the counter holding some tired-looking sausage rolls and sandwiches.

To Charles's query about food, the landlord, who looked like a troll, said they only did snacks. Charles ordered two halves of lager and a couple of sausage rolls. "Not much," he said, carrying the lot back to a table near the door where Agatha was seated. "We'll find something better on the road home."

They ate in silence. "I'll ask the landlord where she lives," said Charles. "Give me her address and I'll find out. Those sausage rolls were disgusting. I wish I hadn't been so hungry." He went to the bar and came back after a few moments. "That was easy. Third cottage on the left."

"I hope she's at home," said Agatha.

The cottage was part of a long terrace with no gardens at the front. They rang the bell and waited. The village seemed strangely silent under the suffocating heat of the day.

At last the door was opened by a tall thin woman with long black hair. She was wearing a faded print dress. She had a large curved nose shadowing a small mouth. But her large green eyes framed by thick lashes were beautiful.

Agatha introduced herself and Charles and stated the reason for her visit. Fiona invited them into a front parlour cluttered with framed photographs of Fiona in every stage of her life. There was a large gilt-framed mirror over the empty fireplace. A sofa and two armchairs were covered in slippery leather.

Fiona sat down. She did not tuck her dress under her and it rode up, exposing the black lace tops of her stockings and a white frilly edge of knickers.

"Poor George." She sighed. "He was so devoted to me."

"I am sure he was," said Charles smoothly.

"Before he died," said Agatha, "he told me he was frightened of some psychopath. Did he say anything to you about being frightened of anyone?"

"No. Everybody loved him."

"And he seems to have loved everybody," said Agatha sourly. "Why did he leave this village?"

"He did it to spare me," said Fiona, throwing her head back in a theatrical gesture.

"From what?"

"A lot of women in the village were silly about him and terribly jealous of me. Some of them were beginning to send me nasty letters. I even had dog shit shoved through my letterbox."

Not more suspects, thought Agatha wearily. She took out a notebook. "Could you please give me their names and addresses?"

"I dare not."

"Give me the name of the worst one," pleaded Agatha.

She chewed her bottom lip. Then she said, "Well, just the one. She was really the worst. Jane Summer. She lives in a cottage along on the right on the other side of the pub. Her cottage is called Tranquility."

"I gather you were having an affair with him," said Agatha bluntly.

Fiona held out a thin hand on which a diamond ring sparkled. "We were engaged to be married."

"So you must have been in constant contact with him," said Charles. "When did you last see him?"

Those large green eyes shifted away from their faces. "He said he was getting a cottage in Carsely ready for us. He said I should stay away until the fuss had died down."

"Would it surprise you to know that he had affairs with several women in Carsely?" asked Agatha.

If she had hoped to rattle Fiona, she failed. Fiona gave her a tolerant smile. "Oh, the same old, same old. Liars all. It would amaze you to know how many of the women in this village claimed the same thing. He used to laugh with me. 'I am devoted to you and you only, Fee,' that's what he'd say."

"Where were you on the day before he was found dead?" asked Charles.

Fiona stood up. "Enough!" she shouted. "You are not the police. Get out of my home."

"Stark, staring bonkers," said Agatha outside. "She's mad enough to have done it."

"She won't see you again," said Charles.

"No, but I'll send someone else." They walked past the pub. Agatha noticed a small sign in the window that said. "Barmaid Wanted."

"I think I'll send Toni to get a job in that pub."

"Wouldn't that put her in danger?"

"No. All she needs to do is pull pints and listen to the village gossip. Oh, here's Jane Summer's cottage. Let's hope this one's sane. I bet she looks awful. I cannot understand George's taste in women."

"He didn't have taste," said Charles brutally. "He would have screwed the cat."

But "dainty" was the word to describe Jane Summer. She was small and pretty with a heart-shaped face and large blue eyes and her curls were genuine blond. She was wearing a man's blouse over denim shorts. Her feet were bare and her toenails painted pink. Agatha judged her to be in her middle thirties.

Agatha explained the reason for their visit and Jane invited them through the house and into her back garden.

"Such a tragedy and so horrible," said Jane. "Have you spoken to Fee?"

"Fiona Morton, yes," said Agatha.

"Horrible woman. She drove him out of the village. She would not leave him alone."

"She said they were engaged and flashed a diamond ring at me," said Agatha.

"I think she probably bought it herself. Fee was an ordinary sort of village lady until George came along and then she seemed to go mad. I hired George to do my garden and she appeared, having climbed over all the intervening fences. George looked terrified. I was so grateful when my husband came home and sent her off."

"Your husband? Where does he work?"

"He's a vet. He has a surgery at the other end of the village. He's often called out to the surrounding farms."

"Where were you on the day before George's body was found?"

"I was here during the day and then, Jack — that's my husband — and I went to a performance at the Playhouse in Oxford. Oh, am I a suspect? I suppose bitchy Fee suggested as much." She went to a desk in the corner of the room and rummaged in a drawer and retrieved a theatre programme and two ticket stubs. "Here's the proof."

"Thank you," said Agatha. "No, I won't take them. The police will be in the village soon, asking questions."

When they left, Charles said, "I'm still hungry. I saw a general store as we drove in. Let's buy some grub and drinks and have a picnic."

The store not only sold sandwiches and hot roast chicken but had a liquor license. Charles bought a bottle of Chardonnay, a chicken, two ham sandwiches and a corkscrew. "We're driving," cautioned Agatha.

" 'We,' paleface? You're driving."

"We should eat it in the car with the air-conditioning on," said Agatha.

"No. A nice breeze has got up. Let's find a shady tree. This is the best summer ever. May as well enjoy it while it lasts."

After the usual irritating search for the perfect place to picnic — "What about there? No, not there. Try farther on," — and when they were on the point of seriously quarrelling, Charles cried, "Stop!"

A little way out of the village, a glassy stream flowed near to the road, and there was a grassy bank shaded by a willow tree.

Agatha, guiltily, had two glasses of wine to accompany the roast chicken and sandwiches. She began to feel sleepy. The stream chuckled past and the long branches of the willow swayed in the breeze. She turned to say something to Charles, but he had fallen neatly asleep. What did he really think of her, she wondered for the umpteenth time. What about that fling they had had in the South of France? It seemed so very long ago and, since then, he had reverted to a casual friendship. Her eyelids drooped and soon she was asleep as well.

She awoke with a start as a large drop of warm rain fell through the willow branches and landed on her nose. "Wake up, Charles," she said, shaking him. "It's beginning to rain." A bright flash of lightning lit up their startled faces and then an enormous crack of thunder seemed to split the sky overhead.

"The sooner we get to the car and away from this tree, the better," said Charles. They hurriedly packed the detritus of their picnic and scrambled into the shelter of the car.

"Home?" asked Charles.

"I don't want to leave here without finding a bit more about Fiona."

"You should leave it to Toni," said Charles lazily. "If she gets the job as barmaid, she'll soon find out more than we could."

Agatha reluctantly agreed. She drove home through the crashing storm and flooded roads. By the time she turned down into the road to Carsely, the rain had stopped and a pale green evening sky was appearing to the west.

She suddenly did not want to spend the rest of the day on her own, but outside her door, Charles said, "Good hunting. Keep me posted," and headed for his car.

Agatha went indoors, petted her cats and checked her phone for messages. There were five from Roy Silver, a former employee of Agatha's, complaining that there was so much publicity about the murder and she might have got him in on it. Roy was a public relations officer who loved, above all, publicity for himself. Agatha phoned him and invited him down for the week-end. Roy was slightly camp, often irritating, but she decided that any company was better than none. Then she wondered what had happened to her former independence, she who had formerly been, she thought, satisfied with her own company.

Charles was about to drive off when someone knocked on the car window. He looked out and saw James Lacey and lowered the window. "I'd like to speak to you," said James. "Have you got a minute?"

"Okay." Charles climbed out of the car and followed James's tall figure into his cottage.

"Drink?" asked James.

"Spit it out," said Charles. "The way you are looking at me reminds me of being up before the headmaster."

"It's just . . . well, what are your intentions as regards to Agatha?"

Charles stared at James's tall, handsome figure in amazement. "Are you joking or are you really as Victorian as you sound?"

"I care for Agatha," said James. "I don't want her hurt."

"My dear fellow," said Charles patiently, "have you not realised that until our Agatha grows up, she's going to continue to fall for weirdos like super Lothario Marston? And take you? If you hadn't been such a confirmed bachelor with 'Unavailable, do not touch' written all over you, she wouldn't have pursued you in the first place."

"I did marry her," said James.

"And what a mess that turned out to be," said Charles ruthlessly. "All we can do is what we have done before and stand on the sidelines of Agatha's life ready to pick up the pieces. You could help her with her detecting like you did before."

"I can't," said James. "I've got to go abroad."

"I thought you'd given up the travel book business."

"It pays the bills. I've been working on a life of Nelson. But that doesn't. Look after Agatha."

"Look, I'm off. I won't hurt Aggie, I promise. So pack your bags and stop worrying."

Chapter Four

Two days later, Toni was ensconced behind the bar of the pub in Lower Sithby, pulling pints. She could hardly believe how easy it had been to get the job. The landlord, Bob Brackett, was certainly only offering the minimum wage, but the job came with a room above the pub. He had not even asked to see Toni's references, which she had faked. He was a thickset, surly man with a slattern of a wife and a squalling baby. He confided in Toni that his wife wouldn't work in the bar anymore.

A friendly barman in Mircester had given Toni a crash course in pulling pints. She had been worried in case anyone would ask for some kind of cocktail, but the regulars were mostly agricultural workers or farmers and all they wanted was pints of beer.

After Toni's first day, the pub began to become crowded as news of the pretty barmaid spread around the village. Wives began to appear to size her up as well as a few of the unmarried village women. The day before she had started work, Phil Marshall had driven down to the village and had snapped a covert photograph of Fiona Morton. Toni kept it in her handbag behind the bar so that she would recognise Fiona if she walked in.

Toni had not seen Simon Black, who, to her annoyance, Agatha had insisted on sending after her to keep an eye on her. She was surprised he had not visited the pub, but was, on the other hand, glad he was keeping away from her. Toni had so far been unable to hear any gossip about Fiona. On Saturday, Toni wondered how Agatha was getting on, interviewing Jessica Fordyce.

Agatha was at that moment wishing with all her heart that she had not invited Roy. That young man refused to leave Agatha to interview Jessica on her own. Jessica was a television star and Roy hoped the press would still be around.

Nothing Agatha could say would persuade him not to wear a pair of emerald green leather shorts and a green open-necked shirt with ballooning sleeves. He had distressingly thin legs ending in green leather ankle boots. He had a fake-bake tan and his hair was highlighted with green and blond stripes. Roy parried every thrust by saying that Agatha was out of touch with fashion.

To Agatha's amazement, she received a friendly welcome from Jessica.

Jessica led them into her kitchen, a miracle of granite tops, copper pans, and gleaming gadgets. Agatha looked round. She had not bothered doing much to her own kitchen, as almost the only appliances in daily use were the microwave and the coffeepot. She remembered when butcher's block kitchen tables had been all the rage and had bought one. But it had a dip in the side to let the blood run down and coffee cups had a habit of sliding down there onto the floor, so she had got rid of it and had bought a conventional one instead. Besides, it had taken a lot of scrubbing to get it clean and Doris Simpson had complained bitterly.

Jessica was wearing a sky blue cotton smock. She was bare legged. She was not wearing any make-up and Agatha noticed there was not a single wrinkle on the beauty of her glowing face. Roy was in raptures. "You're even more gorgeous than you are on the telly," he breathed.

Jessica laughed. "I don't think Agatha came here to worship at my shrine. You're trying to find out who killed George, aren't you?"

"Yes, his sister has retained me," said Agatha. "Have you any idea who would do such a thing?"

"Coffee?"

"Yes, please," said Roy.

Jessica ground beans in an electric grinder and then put the grounds into a coffee machine. "It'll take a few minutes," she said. "Have a seat."

Her hair must be genuine red, thought Agatha, feeling diminished before so much beauty.

They sat round the coffee table. "If you want suspects, you'll need to start with all those village women he was sleeping with," said Jessica.

"You knew about that?" asked Agatha.

Jessica shrugged. "Didn't everyone?"

Except me, thought Agatha bitterly. Jessica, with her open friendly air, was not what Agatha had expected.

"Did you have an affair with him?" asked Agatha.

"No, I recognised his type a mile off."

"And what type is that?"

"I don't think George *liked* women. I think he liked the power. I think he liked easy conquests. I was out of his league." She smiled at Agatha. "I would suppose you were, too."

Agatha warmed to Jessica in that moment. She exuded such a friendly warmth that it was hard not to like her. Roy was gazing at Jessica, his mouth hanging open. Agatha resisted an impulse to lean across and close it for him.

"He mentioned to me that he was afraid of someone who might turn out to be a psychopath. Did he say anything about that to you?" asked Agatha.

Jessica stood up and went to the counter and filled porcelain mugs with coffee. When the coffee was served, she placed a plate of chocolate chip cookies on the table, saying, "Do try them. I baked them."

"Goodness," Roy said, gasping. "You really are a household goddess."

"About the psychopath," said Agatha impatiently. "Roy, you're getting biscuit crumbs down the inside of your shirt!"

"Sorry," said Roy. "But they're so utterly *devoon* that . . ."

"Psychopath," prompted Agatha impatiently.

"No," said Jessica, giving Roy such a dazzling smile that he dropped a biscuit on the floor.

"Sorry, so sorry. I'll get it," babbled Roy.

"Throw it out the back door into the garden for the birds," said Jessica. "Agatha didn't introduce you but I know you. You're Roy Silver. You promoted that band, Get Quick."

"Psychopath!" howled Agatha.

They both stared at her. "I just want to find out who murdered poor George," said Agatha.

Roy gave her a hurt look and made for the kitchen door with the pieces of biscuit.

"No, he didn't," said Jessica. "Did he say whether it was a man or a woman?"

"As a matter of fact, he didn't," said Agatha.

"Then it could be one of the men in the village. George must have caused a lot of jealousy."

"I don't really think so, somehow," said Agatha. "The murder was so vindictive."

"You don't think much of women," commented Jessica.

"Our Aggie is always in competition with the lot of them," said Roy, returning to the table.

Agatha threw him a nasty I'll-speak-to-you-later look from her bearlike eyes.

"I am not," she said. "It's just that one would expect a man to kill him with a shotgun or a blow to the head."

"What are the names of the women he was having affairs with?" asked Jessica.

Agatha hesitated, and then said, "I can't really tell you that at the moment, but if anything breaks, you'll be the first to know."

Jessica laughed. "At least I'm in the clear. I went straight to the ball and left when it was over."

"They think he was killed almost a whole day before," said Agatha.

"Ah! Where was I? I know. I was on location. I'm supposed to be having an affair with one of the doctors."

"I know," breathed Roy. "Giles Deveraux."

"That's the one. And I was facing up to a dirty week-end with him at his cottage in Broadwell — you know, the village with the watersplash, just off the Stow road. We were there all day."

"But you didn't have the affair," said Roy, wriggling with excitement. "You found out he was married."

"You really are a fan," said Jessica.

"You were practically drooling," said Agatha crossly as they walked away from Jessica's cottage some ten minutes later.

"Well, she's gorgeous, and you can rule her out," said Roy.

"Why?"

"She could have any man she wanted. Only an idiot would want to have an affair with the gardener."

"George Marston was a very attractive man," said Agatha. "I'm not writing her off yet. Let's go to Broadwell and ask around."

But in Broadwell, they found out that the cast of the hospital soap had been there for the whole day, but had packed up in the early evening. "That still gives her time," said Agatha.

"Use your head," snapped Roy waspishly. "She would need to be carrying a bag of snakes around with her. Anyway, they all drove off back to London. You're letting jealousy blind you, Aggie."

"I am not!" raged Agatha, and they quarrelled all the way back to her cottage and they were still quarrelling by the time Roy took his leave.

Simon had found a cheap room in a bed and breakfast in the village. He said he was spending time in the Oxfordshire villages, claiming London as his home and saying he needed some fresh air. His landlady, a Mrs. Greta James, was a cheerful gossipy woman so Simon soon heard all about the new pretty barmaid at the pub. He did not want to ask outright about Fiona Morton, but he had a copy of one of Phil's photographs of her. He was just wondering whether he would ever manage a chance meeting when one morning, he saw Fiona leave her cottage and head for the village store. Simon raced past her, bought a loaf in the store, and managed to "accidentally" collide with her as she was about to enter.

"I am so sorry," he said. "But it's not every day I bump into an attractive lady."

"Watch where you're going next time," said Fiona, and made to move past him.

"Look!" said Simon. "I really am most awfully sorry. May I buy you a drink?"

He gazed at her with adoring eyes, hoping he wasn't laying it on too thick. She appeared to survey him properly for the first time, from his thatch of thick black hair to his jester's face and sturdy body.

"Well," she said, suddenly coy. "I suppose one little drink would start the day. I don't usually go there. Full of rough types. Everyone's talking about some new barmaid."

"Let's go anyway," urged Simon. "I'll protect you."

She took his arm and smiled at him. They walked together into the pub. Behind the bar, Toni glowed in the dimness of the old pub. Fiona looked as if she had suddenly sucked several lemons. "So that's the new barmaid," she said. "I believe she is considered beautiful. Can't see it myself."

"No use asking me," said Simon cheerfully. "I prefer maturity. What'll you have to drink?"

"Vodka and tonic, please." Simon held out a chair for her in a corner and then went to the bar. "A half pint of lager and a large vodka and tonic, miss," he ordered.

"Right, sir, coming up," said Toni. She murmured, "That her?"

"In the scrawny flesh."

"Be careful."

"Meet me later. We need to exchange notes."

"Don't get off until eleven in the evening. Where?"

"Have you seen that ruined church just outside the north of the village?"

"I know the one."

"I'll be there just after eleven."

During this conversation they had barely moved their lips. Simon returned with the drinks.

"I'd better introduce myself. I'm Simon White."

"And I'm Fiona Morton, but my friends call me Fee."

"Fee it is," said Simon.

"And what brings you to our little village?"

Simon talked about wanting to get out of

London for a break. "I'm in advertising," he lied. "Very stressful. Too many boozy lunches. I'm a copywriter. Are you a lady of leisure?"

"For my sins. Dear Papa left me quite well off. But I am very involved in village activities."

A ray of sun penetrating through the dusty window sent prisms of light sparkling on Fiona's diamond ring.

"Oh, you're engaged," said Simon. "Who's the lucky fellow?"

"It's a great tragedy. He loved me so much and now he's dead."

"I am so sorry. What did he die of?"

"He was murdered!"

"No! How ghastly. How did it happen?"

"His name was George Marston. He had moved to a Cotswold village to prepare a home for us when he was struck down."

"You mean a blow on the head?"

"I do not know yet how he died."

Nothing about adders, thought Simon. But there had been nothing about that part of the murder in the newspapers.

"You must be devastated," he said.

"I am. I have cried and cried until I can cry no more."

Her eyes were really beautiful, thought Simon. Green like large emeralds. Pity about the rest of her.

"Another drink," he offered.

"Just a little one."

The pub was filling up. Toni had been joined behind the bar by the landlord and it was he who took Simon's order.

When he returned with the drinks, Fiona gave him a watery smile. "I've been having a teeny sob," she said. "So hard to get over."

"When did you last see George?"

"Why do you ask?" she demanded, her eyes suspicious.

"My dear Fee," said Simon earnestly. "I have no desire to pry into your personal life. I know. Why don't I take you out for dinner to cheer you up? Is there anywhere good near here?"

"How very kind. There's nothing in the village, of course, but Chez Henri is only twenty miles away. Have you heard of it?"

"Oh, yes," said Simon. Chez Henri was a restaurant run by two French chefs and set in an old manor house in the Oxford countryside. He had heard it was very expensive. Still, all in a good cause.

He smiled at her. "I'll book a table if I can get one. Eight o'clock?"

"Wonderful. I'll point out my cottage to you."

Simon phoned Toni as soon as Fiona had

gone and cancelled their appointment for that evening.

Agatha sat in her garden that evening before going to bed. Simon had phoned her earlier about his dinner engagement. She could only hope it would turn out to be worth the expense. She felt uneasy. She had gone to the village shop earlier that evening to buy some cat food and had been made aware of a hostile attitude towards her from the customers in the shop. Nothing was said but she received some nasty looks.

She stifled a yawn and decided to go to bed. She noticed her cats had not touched their bowls of cat food. They had been thoroughly spoilt and obviously expected their usual diet of fresh fish or liver.

"I haven't time to pamper you," said Agatha. "Try to eat the stuff." And avoiding her cats' accusing eyes, she went up to prepare to go to bed.

She had just put on her nightdress when she heard her cats begin to howl and hiss.

"Snakes and bastards," shouted Agatha. "It's cat food, not poison."

She decided to go downstairs to see if she could calm them down. Hodge and Boswell were sitting staring at the door, their cries rending the air.

"What?" began Agatha, and then she became aware of an evil smell. She looked down and noticed a pile of what looked like excrement which had been shoved through her letterbox. All of it had fortunately landed on the doormat. Agatha got a strong rubbish bag and tipped the doormat into it and then got spray cleaner and cleaned the letterbox and what was smeared inside of her front door.

She dumped the rubbish bag in the bin at the bottom of her back garden. When she returned to the house, she found her hands were shaking. Agatha phoned the police and sat down and waited.

Bill Wong was just about to go off duty when he heard of Agatha's call. "I'll see her," he said, and set out for Carsely.

Agatha let him in. "There's something going on, Bill," she cried. "I was at the store earlier and you could have cut the atmosphere with a knife. I can't phone Mrs. Bloxby because it's too late."

"Normally, we wouldn't do anything about this," said Bill, "as we haven't the resources. But as this is a murder enquiry, I'll send forensics along in the morning to see if they can get any fingerprints off your front door. Was the shit human or animal?"

"Don't know," said Agatha. "Smelled dire."

"Where did you dump it?"

"It was practically all on the doormat so I scooped up the doormat, put it in a rubbish bag and dumped it in the bin."

"Show me."

Agatha unlocked the kitchen door and led him down the garden to the bin. The garden was fragrant with all the flowers George had planted. She had a sudden vivid picture of him working away.

Bill opened the bin, shone his torch into it and sniffed.

"Pooh! That's pig manure, Agatha. Someone could get it anywhere around here. Lock up and go to bed and we'll see what we can do for you tomorrow."

After an uneasy night's sleep, Agatha phoned Mrs. Bloxby and explained what had happened. "I'll be round right away," said the vicar's wife.

While she waited for her, Agatha phoned the office and told them why she would be late that day.

When Mrs. Bloxby arrived, Agatha said, "Who on earth would do such a thing?"

"I sometimes think when something riles the villagers up, they go back mentally two hundred years," said Mrs. Bloxby.

"Let's sit in the garden so I can smoke," said Agatha. "Tell me what you mean. I was down in the village store yesterday and was treated like Typhoid Mary."

"There are nasty rumours," said Mrs. Bloxby cautiously.

"About me?"

"Do you know Mrs. Arnold, an elderly lady who does the flowers in the church?"

"I've seen her around. What about her?"

"I met her in church yesterday and she told me I ought to keep clear of you. She said she had it on good authority that you had killed George Marston yourself. I said that was ridiculous. Mrs. Arnold said that everyone in the village knew that even if you hadn't killed Mr. Marston, you had brought evil to the village because of your record of hunting down murderers.

"The trouble about these Cotswold villages, even though they are full of newcomers, I swear there is something in the very stones that make people revert to witch hunting."

"Did she say who the good authority was?" Agatha asked.

"She said she had never been one to gossip."

"Typical," snorted Agatha. "How do I counteract this? It's going to make interviewing people in the village almost impossible."

"You are the public relations expert. If you were advising a client, what would you tell them to do?"

Agatha scowled in thought. Then her face cleared. "The press, of course. They'll be interested in anything to do with the murders."

"That might make it worse," said Mrs. Bloxby cautiously.

"How?"

"Naturally reporters will want to interview the villagers. You might be handing some nasty people a free platform."

"Damn! I'll face them down myself. I'll run off fliers on my printer and call a meeting in the village hall this evening."

"Will they come?"

"When I say on the flier it's about the murder of George Marston, they'll come, all right."

The village hall was packed that evening as Agatha stood up before the microphone. She had been disappointed the police had not found any fingerprints on her door. Whoever had put the pig manure through her letterbox had worn gloves.

To make sure of a big audience, she had

also advertised a free wine bar.

She cleared her throat and looked down at the sea of faces. She noticed that Joyce Hemingway, Sarah Freemantle and Harriet Glossop were seated together in the front row.

"Ladies and gentlemen," she began, "someone in this village has murdered George Marston."

There was a shocked silence.

"And to turn the blame away from themselves, they have tried to blacken my name and also, to intimidate me. Someone shoved pig manure through my letterbox, a silly, spiteful thing to do. If you listen to these rumours and give them credence, then you are protecting a murderer or" — she glared down at the front row — "a murderess. I am employed by Mr. Marston's sister to discover the identity of this vicious killer.

"I want anyone in this hall who knows anything that might help my investigation to come and tell me. Listening to these rumours and starting a sort of witch hunt against me is playing into someone's hands. Do any of you know, for example, someone who was trying to get hold of pig manure? Does anyone know of anyone who might know how to handle snakes?

"Someone is blaming me for bringing this

evil into Carsely. I did not bring it. The murderer did. All this vendetta against me is doing is delaying me finding out the identity of the murderer.

"The bar is now open."

Chairs were scraped back. The villagers headed for a long table at the rear of the hall where there was a buffet of wine and cheese.

Agatha stepped down from the platform and went to the toilet to repair her make-up. When she emerged, Phil Marshall was waiting for her.

"I've been asking around," he said, "but I'm blessed if I can find out the source of the nasty gossip. Someone'll say something like it was Jim Bloggs who told me and Jim Bloggs will say he got it from Old Uncle Tom Cobbley and so it goes."

Agatha's eyes raked the crowd. "Where have Freemantle, Hemingway and Glossop gone?"

"I was watching them for their reactions. They were very subdued and left the hall immediately after your speech was over."

"My money's on Joyce Hemingway," said Agatha.

Various villagers came up to her then to explain they had nothing to do with the malicious gossip and then settled down to enjoy the free booze and have a party.

Agatha was tired when the evening was at last over but felt she had at least achieved her aim.

She had just let herself into her cottage when her phone rang. It was Simon.

"How long do I have to go on with this?" he asked plaintively.

Agatha had been so busy startling the villagers by saying the murderer was one of them that she had almost forgotten about Fiona Morton.

"Why? Nothing useful?"

"No, and she seems to be transferring her obsession for George to me. I took her to that posh restaurant. All nouvelle cuisine. I tell you, I could have put the pudding in my eye and used it as a monocle, it was so small. Fiona tried to get me to come into her cottage for a nightcap. I said I was tired. She demanded a good-night kiss. You'd never think a woman with such a small mouth should have such a large tongue. Yuk!"

"How's Toni getting on?"

"I managed to meet up with her to compare notes. All she's found out is that our Fiona is considered a bit of a nutcase. But one good bit of info. George was supposed to have been murdered at least twenty-four hours before the ball. Right?"

"So the police say."

"Well, Fiona was on the committee of the local fete and she was working on the arrangements the day before and on the day of the murder. Her car never left the village."

Agatha sighed. "You'd better both get out of there. Is Toni sure there is no way she could have sneaked off?"

"Quite sure."

"You'd better both get out of there," she repeated.

"Toni will be glad to go. The landlord's been paying her off the books, so she didn't need to give her correct name. Also, she said the vet, Summers, has taken to dropping in and keeps saying he's sure he's seen her somewhere before. Her photo has been in the newspapers in the past."

"Pack up and leave this evening," said Agatha. "What about George romancing any other women in that village?"

"It seems to have been wishful thinking. Can you imagine such stupidity?"

"Goodbye," said Agatha abruptly.

Simon heaved a sigh of relief as he rang off. He pulled his suitcase out from under the bed and began to pack. When he was finished packing, he looked down from his window and drew back quickly. Fiona was standing in the street, looking up at his window.

Simon retreated from the window and switched off the light. He sat on the bed and waited for half an hour before cautiously looking out again. Fiona had gone.

He telephoned Toni on her mobile and asked her how quickly she could leave. "When are you going?" Toni asked.

"As soon as possible," said Simon. "That Fiona is beginning to terrify me."

"I just have a backpack. I can drop it out of the window and then climb down after it. My car's in the car park, but the ground is on a slope, so I can let out the brake and cruise quietly onto the road. See you in the office tomorrow."

"Wait a bit," protested Simon. "Don't you think we deserve a day off? We could go somewhere nice."

"No. See you at work."

Agatha slept well that night, feeling that she had scotched all the animosity towards her. But she awoke the next morning feeling heavy and sweaty. She looked out of the window. The sky was the colour of pewter. Not a leaf moved in the garden. The air was sticky and close. She showered and put on a cotton blouse and a cotton skirt with an elasticated waist. Just for one day, she thought, I do not want to be reminded about my waistline every time I eat.

After her usual breakfast of two cups of black coffee and two cigarettes, she unlocked her front door, ready to go to the office. There was a parcel on her doorstep. It was a plain brown paper parcel with her name printed on it in block capitals. She stared down at it. Then she went back indoors and phoned the police.

Bill Wong and Alice Peterson arrived three-quarters of an hour later. They examined the parcel while Agatha described the recent hate campaign against her in the village. "I thought it was all over," she wailed.

"It might be something innocent," said Bill.

"Well, you open it!" said Agatha.

"I'm going to go ahead," said Bill. "You and Alice had better leave the kitchen. I really don't think it's a bomb."

"We'll be in the garden," said Agatha, shooing her cats outside to safety.

She and Alice waited anxiously while the cats chased each other over the grass. I wonder if there is such a thing as reincarnation, thought Agatha. I wouldn't mind coming back as a cat. But what if I ended up in a home with ghastly children who would torture me?

Bill opened the kitchen door. "You can come in now. It's safe."

Alice and Agatha walked into the kitchen. Bill had removed the brown paper wrapping to reveal a box of Belgian chocolates. A pink card was on top of the box. It read, "Best wishes from Carsely."

"There you are," said Bill. "False alarm."

"I still don't like it," said Agatha. "Look! The box has been sealed on either side with bits of Scotch tape. I don't think it was like that in the shop."

Bill took out a penknife and slit the tape. He lifted the lid of the box and then removed the quilted white paper that covered the top of the chocolates.

He let out a cry of alarm. An adder slid out of the box, and, in front of their horrified eyes, slid rapidly across the table, dropped to the floor and sped out into the garden.

"My cats!" shrieked Agatha, running into the garden.

"Come back!" yelled Bill as Agatha frantically chased her cats around the garden, trying to catch them. But Hodge and Boswell thought it was a new game and kept racing away from her.

Bill and Alice seized Agatha and marched her back into the kitchen. "Sit down, you silly woman," roared Bill. "I'll get on to headquarters. We need a snake handler and a forensic team."

Agatha tempted her cats indoors with a packet of pate and sat shivering with shock despite the heat of the day. She retreated to her living room with her cats as the house filled up with men in white suits and a snake handler who began to search the garden.

Alice Peterson followed her in and took down a statement. Agatha had just finished speaking when they heard a cry: "Got it!"

Agatha went through to the kitchen, where the snake handler was holding a bag. "Your adder is nearly dead," he said. "Might have been fed something to tranquillise it and get it into the box and been given too much. Of course, adders are in trouble. There's been a lot of inbreeding and some of them are dying off. Pity."

"What do you mean 'pity'?" raged Agatha. "It would relieve my mind if the whole lot perished."

"Now, now," admonished the snake handler. "They're God's creatures."

"I don't care if it's dead," said Agatha. "Just get it out of here!"

The snake handler had a freckled face and sandy hair. His wide blue eyes looked at Agatha with disapproval. "This is Britain's last venomous snake and we will do all we can to preserve it. We are taking DNA swabs of adders and moving them to different locations to stop inbreeding. So many of their natural habitats have been destroyed."

"I repeat," said Agatha through gritted teeth, "get it out of here." She retreated to the sitting room and asked Alice if she might go to the local pub and leave the police to do their work. "You have my mobile number," said Agatha. "You can phone me when you are finished."

Alice checked with Bill and then returned to give Agatha permission.

In the garden of the Red Lion, Agatha phoned the newspapers and television and gave them the story and said she was at the Red Lion and would be available for interviews.

No point in forgoing good publicity for her agency.

It was late afternoon by the time all the interviews were over. As Agatha was walking back to her cottage, she received a phone call from Alice to say that they were all leaving.

Bill was waiting on the doorstep. "We

might get something off the package. I'll let you know. Can't get any footprints off the path."

"What have you been doing all day?" asked Agatha.

"Questioning people in the village. Dead loss. No one saw anything and James is away. It might be a good idea if you moved out for a bit."

"I won't be driven out of my home," said Agatha stubbornly.

CHAPTER FIVE

Fiona Morton was very upset when she found out that Simon had disappeared in the middle of the night, and, what made matters worse in her mind, was that the pretty barmaid had disappeared at the same time.

She was engulfed with fury. She convinced herself that he had been leading her on and thirsted for revenge.

Simon had been gone for two days when retired policeman Jeff Lindsey opened the door of his cottage in Lower Sithby and found Fiona on the doorstep.

"What do you want, Fee?" he demanded ungraciously. He was an elderly man with thick grey hair and a rather weak face. He had been the village policeman in Lower Sithby for years but had been forcibly retired when the previous government had started to sell off village police stations.

"Let me in," ordered Fiona. "I need

your help."

Jeff stood aside reluctantly and Fiona strode past him into his cluttered living room and sat down on a sofa.

"It's like this, Jeff. I want to sue someone for breach of promise."

"You mean that young fellow you've been seen around with?"

"Yes, him. I have the registration of his car and I want you to find out who he is."

"I'm retired," protested Jeff.

"But you have contacts. When Josh Barton up at the farm wanted you to check on a couple who were renting his holiday cottage, you did that for him."

Jeff sighed. He knew unless he did what Fiona wanted, she would never leave him in peace.

"Give me a couple of hours," he said.

Fiona left him and went back to her cottage, where she sat and fretted. How could Simon have treated her so shabbily?

She drank vodka and stared at the clock, willing it to move faster. When two hours were up, she made her way back to Jeff's cottage.

He handed her a slip of paper. "That car is registered to a Simon Black. That's his address. He lives in Mircester."

Fiona wasted no time. She got into her

car and drove to Mircester, where she bought a street map and then consulted the address again — 5, Mill Lane.

Mill Lane was a winding narrow street at the back of the abbey. Number five was a former mews house, trim and expensive looking. So Simon must have money.

He'll need all of it by the time the courts and I have finished with him, thought Fiona grimly.

But first, she was determined to find out more about him. She parked outside his house and waited. A thin drizzle was falling, smearing the windscreen of her car. The long day dragged on until evening. The street lamps came on. Her eyes were just beginning to droop and she was feeling very hungry when, glancing in her rearview mirror, she saw the familiar figure of Simon, lit by a street lamp, approaching his front door.

Fiona was about to get out and confront him when she suddenly decided it would be better to find out where he worked. It would be interesting to see what his bosses would think of him when she challenged him.

She found a small bed and breakfast place nearby and took a room, explaining that she did not have any luggage because she had missed the last train. Setting her travelling alarm for seven in the morning, she tried to get some sleep, but the abbey clock was very loud and not only chimed the hour during the night but the half hours and quarter hours.

By the time her alarm went off, she was feeling ragged and hungrier than ever. The woman who ran the bed and breakfast had agreed to supply her with an early-morning meal. Fiona ate ravenously, drank three cups of coffee and felt ready for battle.

Simon looked out of his window in the morning. There was a Peugeot parked outside his door. He remembered it had been there with the engine running the night before. Then the sun, peeping over the rooftops, lit up the face of Fiona Morton behind the wheel.

He cursed under his breath. How on earth had that terrifying woman found out where he lived? He dressed hurriedly and left by his small back garden and out into a lane that ran along the back. Then he hurried to the office, where he told Agatha that Fiona Morton was stalking him.

"What were you up to?" asked Agatha. "Didn't have an affair with her, did you?"

"No!"

"Let me think. You'd better move into a bed and breakfast until she gets tired," said

Agatha. "Give your keys to Patrick and he'll go home and pack some clothes for you."

"You'll need to go in the back way," said Simon, handing over his keys. "She's watching the front."

Three hours later, Fiona angrily rang the doorbell. No reply. She stood, irresolute. Then she went to the library and looked up the yellow pages for a detective agency. She would put experts on the chase.

Fiona settled on the Agatha Raisin Detective Agency. A woman would be sympathetic to her plight.

Agatha was just about to leave her office to go back to Carsely and start interviewing the villagers herself in the hope that someone had been seen carrying that box of chocolates towards her cottage.

She looked up as the door opened and Fiona walked in. Agatha recognised her immediately from her meeting with her. She could only be glad that both Toni and Simon were out.

Fiona burst into a speech about how she wanted to find Simon and sue him for breach of promise. Agatha listened in growing alarm and then, when Fiona had finished, she said, "Have you a letter from him? Have you anything except your word to show his intentions were serious?"

"No, but . . ."

"You can try other detective agencies, you can try lawyers," said Agatha, "but they will all tell you the same thing. You have absolutely no proof of any serious commitment. In fact, I don't know of any successful breach-of-promise case. It's not as if you're an underage teenager. No one is going to take you seriously.

"Didn't you recently claim to me that George Marston wanted to marry you?"

"Yes, yes he did," said Fiona passionately. "He went to Carsely to set up a home for us."

"Mr. Marston not only gardened in Carsely but bedded a few of the local women. He was in the village before his death for a good few months. I'm willing to bet he did not contact you once."

"That's not true! He phoned me everyday."

"Mrs. Ilston, George's sister, gave your name as a possible suspect. The police have that name. They will be checking your phone records and they will have checked George Marston's phone records."

"You nasty bitch! I'll . . . I'll . . ."

"You'll what?" demanded Agatha brutally. "Get out of here and stop wasting my time.

Instead of looking for a lawyer, I suggest you contact a psychiatrist."

Fiona's face turned a muddy colour. She had advanced threateningly on Agatha just as the door opened and Patrick walked in.

"Miss Morton was just leaving," said Agatha.

"You haven't heard the last of me," raged Fiona.

"I sincerely hope I have," said Agatha as the door crashed behind Fiona.

Fiona marched to the central car park where she had left her vehicle. She was just about to get into it when she saw Toni — the barmaid! — drive up. She locked her car again and followed the girl. Toni went straight to the detective agency.

Now Fiona's fury knew no bounds. That wretched Raisin woman probably had Simon as well as Toni working for her, and all Simon had been doing was smooching up to her to find out if she was a murderess. And what had that wretched woman said about her darling George having affairs in Carsely?

She went to the nearest pub and drank several vodkas, her hatred of Agatha and Simon mounting with each glass. I am, she decided tipsily, a woman of action. I will go to this wretched village, find out where that Raisin woman lives and force her to listen to me.

Fiona returned to her car and took out an ordnance survey map of Gloucestershire. But the lines swam before her eyes. Soon she was asleep. She awoke hours later with her head resting against the steering wheel.

Remembering her mission, she consulted the map again and, this time, located the route to Carsely. Still feeling the effects of all she had drunk, she drove slowly and carefully, finally reaching Carsely.

Fiona parked in front of the general store. A stout elderly woman with a sour face was just leaving. "Do you have Agatha Raisin's address?" asked Fiona, putting on what she thought was a winsome smile. Had the woman been anyone else but Mrs. Arnold, Fiona would probably have been asked her business, but Mrs. Arnold, looking at Fiona's deranged face, hoped to make trouble.

"It's Lilac Lane, over there," said Mrs. Arnold. "The thatched cottage at the end."

Fiona marched off, weaving her way towards Lilac Lane, the effects of all she had drunk having not yet worn off.

She rang the bell and hammered on the door but there was no reply. She stood back and looked around. The leafy lane seemed to swim in the sunlight. She saw a path at the side of the house. She found her way blocked by a padlocked gate. She climbed nimbly over it.

Fiona settled herself on a garden chair, determined to wait. The sun was hot but she was wearing a wide-brimmed straw hat. She looked sourly at the blaze of flowers. No doubt George's work. She felt a stab of vicious jealousy. The day was warm and her eyelids began to droop again. Her head fell on her bosom, her hat tipped over her face, and she fell asleep and began to snore. Fiona slept so deeply that a figure climbing over the garden fence and dropping to the ground did not wake her.

Agatha arrived home an hour later. Her cats ran in front of her to the garden door and Boswell started pawing at it and meowing. She experienced a sudden spasm of fear. Were there snakes out there?

She looked cautiously through the glass panes of the door. A woman was seated at the garden table, her head covered by a large hat. The hat was black and red. Agatha was about to open the door when she suddenly saw how that red colour glittered unnaturally in the sunlight.

With trembling hands, she seized the phone receiver and called the police. Then she slowly sank down on the floor and hugged her knees.

The front doorbell rang shrilly. Surely not the police so soon. She heaved herself to her feet and went to the door and peered through the spyhole. Charles Fraith was standing outside. Agatha opened the door, stared at Charles and burst into tears.

He wrapped his arms around her. "What's happened?" Agatha gulped and pulled herself together. "In the garden," she said. "I think she's dead."

Charles released her and strode into the house and straight out into the garden. Agatha hurried after him, crying, "Don't touch anything! The police are coming!"

Charles returned to the kitchen. "Do you recognise her?"

"I can't see anything. That hat is right over her eyes. Wait a moment. Where have I seen those black lace tights before? My God! It's Fiona Morton!"

"You're sure?"

"Pretty sure. She called at the office today. She'd tracked me down. She must have been waiting for me. They'll think I murdered her."

"Got an alibi? Calm down and think."

"Let me see. I left the office at seven and then I went to the pub for a snack. I left there just after eight o'clock."

"Good. Relax, they'll probably find at the post mortem that she was dead before you got home."

"I need a large drink."

"I think hot sweet tea is a better idea."

"I'm sure it is, but a large gin and tonic is an even better one."

"Okay. Sit down and stop fretting. I'll get it for you."

Agatha watched his well-barbered hair and immaculate-clothed figure heading towards her sitting room and wondered, not for the first time, how Charles, with his privileged background, could remain so calm.

He returned with a gin and tonic for Agatha and a whisky for himself just as they both heard the wail of sirens in the distance.

Agatha, after she had identified the body as that of Fiona Morton, found herself a prime suspect. Ever since the murder of George Marston, the police had been busy asking questions around the village and had learned of Agatha's infatuation with George. Wilkes promptly decided that Agatha had brained the woman in a jealous rage.

She was taken off to police headquarters

for questioning. She was forced to tell them about sending Simon to investigate and about how Fiona had found out and had visited her at the detective agency. She gave her alibi, which was checked while the questioning went on and on. Agatha had been out of favour with the police before, but never to such an extent, especially when her alibi checked out. Balked of his prey, Wilkes gave her a blistering lecture about having interfered in police business, told her not to leave the country, and finally dismissed her.

Agatha emerged wearily into the reception area to find Charles waiting for her with a suitcase and a travel bag. "The place is crawling with forensic people and coppers," he said. "I gave your cats to Doris and we're clearing off to a hotel. I booked us rooms at the George."

"Thanks," said Agatha. "That was good of you. I'm starving and it's pretty late. Most of the restaurants close at nine thirty."

"There's a curry house opposite the George or we can get sandwiches at the hotel."

"Sandwiches, I think. I don't feel like being out in public because I've just had a nasty thought."

"Which is?"

"Fiona had that stupid large hat covering her face. What if someone thought she was me?"

"That did cross my mind, but I didn't want to worry you."

"I should tell them."

"Leave it. I'll phone Bill when we get to the hotel."

They were in the small sitting room adjoining the bedroom in Agatha's suite at the hotel, finishing a plate of egg and cress sandwiches, when Bill Wong arrived.

"I couldn't make it earlier, Charles," he said. "Do you really think someone might have been out to murder Agatha?"

"They tried to kill her before. Why not now?" asked Charles.

Bill flipped open his notebook. "Let's see. George was rumoured to have had affairs with these women: Joyce Hemingway, Harriet Glossop and Sarah Freemantle."

"My money's on Joyce Hemingway," said Agatha bitterly. "Acidulous cow!"

"But Harriet Glossop is the only one with a record."

"Surely not," said Agatha. "The only drama in that woman's life, I'd have sworn, is when her angel cakes failed to rise in the oven. What did she do?"

"Harriet Glossop was suspected of having killed her first husband."

"Her *first* husband!" Life is not fair, thought Agatha. After all the tints and nonsurgical facelifts I've undergone, a woman who looks like a cottage loaf goes out there and gets more than one husband — forgetting that she had already had two herself. "What did she do?" she asked aloud.

"He took an overdose of barbiturates. There was no suicide note. Harriet was suspected. At last it came out that the silly woman had the suicide note all along but was ashamed of having a husband who had committed suicide over an affair with another woman."

"Maybe she wrote it herself," said Agatha.

"Agatha! A handwriting expert checked it. It's my belief that someone in that village thinks more highly of your detective capabilities than Wilkes does."

"What about Jessica Fordyce?"

"Ironclad alibis. Agatha, she only comes down at week-ends. I think you should go away for a long holiday until we clear this up."

"I'm not running away," said Agatha, wishing in that moment that she hadn't got so much unhealthy pride. It would be lovely to clear off and feel safe again.

"Well, concentrate on your other cases. Keep clear of the press. I think the more high profile you are, the greater the danger."

"How's Alice Peterson?"

Bill's almond-shaped eyes in his round face lit up. "Oh, she's wonderful. So pretty and great to work with."

Agatha felt jealous. Bill was her first friend when she moved to the Cotswolds and, although he was considerably younger than she was, she felt possessive of him.

"Any romance?"

"It's against the rules."

"What rules?" asked Charles. "I bet it happens all the time."

"I don't want to spoil things. Leave my private life alone. Agatha, you've to come back to headquarters tomorrow. They want to question you further."

"Snakes and bastards," groaned Agatha.

When Bill had gone, Charles helped himself to a whisky from the minibar and settled down to watch television. He switched to a showing of *CSI: Miami.*

"I've had enough crime for one day," complained Agatha.

"But this is fictional crime," protested Charles.

There was a shot on the screen of a long

sandy beach. "Sometimes," said Agatha, "when things are bad, I wish I could just walk right into the television screen and take time off from reality. I don't mean be part of the plot, but just stand somewhere sunny and watch them filming."

"Then it might be a good idea to take Bill's advice and go away. You could be walking on a beach somewhere tomorrow."

"You forget, I've been told not to leave the country."

"There are beaches in Britain."

"Pah and pooh to you. I'm going to bed. Switch off the TV when you leave."

It was late afternoon the next day, and after a tedious few hours of questioning, Agatha was able to go home. She was furious with Charles. He had left early that morning, leaving her to pay the whole hotel bill for both of them. She picked up her cats from Doris, went to her cottage, let the cats out into the garden, and settled down with a sigh to read the post, which had arrived in her absence.

She threw the junk mail in the kitchen bin, put the bills to one side, and found a handwritten envelope with the postmark Wyckhadden.

Agatha remembered how, during a case

there, she had become engaged to the local chief inspector, Jimmy Jessop, who had subsequently broken off the engagement after finding her in bed with Charles. Fickle, faithless Charles! Jimmy had subsequently married a local woman, said he was happy, and that was the end of that.

She slit open the envelope and read:

Dear Agatha,

I have been reading about you in the newspapers and you seem to be having an awful time. I have been through the wars as well. My poor wife died of cancer last year.

If you ever feel in need of a holiday, I can put you up. Crime is slack here so I'd be able to take you around.

Keep in touch!

Yours affectionately,
Jimmy

Agatha read the letter over again. Perhaps it would be nice to take a break and get the hell out of Carsely. But that might leave Toni in peril. This murderer might decide to punish her by attacking Toni. And what about Harriet Glossop?

I should really interview her again, thought Agatha. But at police headquarters, they had told her that Fiona's attacker had climbed over the high cedar wood fence that bordered that side of Agatha's garden. Harriet was round and motherly and surely not fit enough to scale that fence.

And what of Jessica Fordyce and her cast-iron alibis? Surely that in itself was suspicious. Innocent people usually had a hard time accounting for their movements. Then there was Joyce Hemingway — thin, stringy and athletic.

But back to Sarah Freemantle. Where was Mr. Freemantle? Could he have returned from the rigs a jealous man? What was he like? Had Sarah been telling the truth when she had said she had not had an affair with George?

There was a ring at the doorbell. Agatha peered nervously through the spyhole and gave a sigh of relief as she recognised the mild features of the vicar's wife. She swung the door wide open, and cried, "Come in!"

"I heard the news about Miss Morton," said Mrs. Bloxby, walking with Agatha into the kitchen. "How horrible for you! Don't you feel you ought to get away?"

"Read this while I make some coffee," said Agatha, handing her Jim's letter.

Mrs. Bloxby read it carefully. Here was a respectable widower, she thought. Surely just the thing. She pictured Agatha married and settled down in a seaside town far from danger.

"This would make a nice break for you," she said. "Why not just go down for the week-end and get away from all this? You surely cannot think very clearly about the murders when you seem to be under threat yourself. I thought they might at least have put a police guard on your door."

"It wouldn't surprise me if Wilkes hopes I *will* get bumped off," said Agatha. "Has anyone heard anything of the estranged Mr. Glossop?"

"Yes, he arrived yesterday."

"Aha!" said Agatha, putting the coffeepot down on the table.

"Now, Mrs. Raisin. I know Mr. Glossop and he seems a very respectable man."

"Why did they break up?"

"I am not sure. I think I remember hearing it was an amicable separation."

"I think I should go and see him. Biscuits?"

Mrs. Bloxby sighed. She feared for her friend.

After Mrs. Bloxby had left, Agatha set off to the Glossops' home, driving her car, because she was nervous of walking, feeling there were adders lurking everywhere. The sky above was bright blue and the sun shone remorselessly down on the drooping flowers in the gardens. I'd better hire a gardener to water mine, thought Agatha. Doris's promised gardener has not turned up. I sometimes wish I had only a window box to bother about. That's the problem of living in a cottagey countryside. Everyone expected you to have a garden stuffed with flowers.

She parked her Mercedes Smart Car in a small space outside the Glossops' cottage, blessing the tiny car, not for the first time, because Agatha could not parallel park.

She got out from the air-conditioned car and the heat engulfed her. A tall, thin, wiry man was working in the front garden, watering the plants. Obviously Mr. Glossop had decided to ignore the hosepipe ban.

"Mr. Glossop."

"Can I help you?"

"I am Agatha Raisin. . . ."

"The village's nosey parker? Get lost."

"Just a few questions."

"Shove off!"

Agatha retreated. She was just about to get into her car when she saw the dumpy figure of Harriet Glossop at the end of the road. She moved quickly to meet her, hoping to have a few words with her out of sight of her husband.

Harriet was wearing a brief pair of shorts. Her legs were very hairy and, as she stopped in front of Agatha and raised a hand to wipe her brow, she revealed a bunch of thick brown hair under her armpit.

Goodness, thought Agatha, to think of all the time I've spent getting waxed and dewerewolfed, and yet George would not even consider an affair with me!

Harriet short-sightedly blinked in the sunlight. She took a pair of glasses out of the pocket of her sleeveless blouse and focussed on Agatha. "Oh, it's you."

"Where were you late yesterday afternoon?" said Agatha.

"I've already told the police. Round and about the village. Now, if you don't mind . . ."

She sprinted past Agatha, running with nimble ease.

Our Harriet's athletic, thought Agatha. She could have scaled my fence.

She got into her car and wondered whether to see Joyce Hemingway and Sarah Freemantle. But the police would have already checked on their alibis. Better to let Patrick Mulligan try to find out something from his police contacts.

Agatha drove to her office in Mircester. Toni was typing out a report while Simon sat beside her drinking coffee. Two electric fans whirred busily.

"Where's Mrs. Freedman?" asked Agatha.

"She was feeling faint with the heat," said Toni. "She's gone home. Simon and I have just had a good result on the Bramley divorce case. How are you bearing up?"

"All right, but not getting anywhere fast."

"Do you want Simon and me to have a go at it?" asked Toni.

"That might be an idea, but do be careful. I'll give you the file and photographs. Phil was able to sneak photos of the suspects. Maybe the murder of Fiona has nothing to do with George's murder. Maybe the killer didn't think it was me after all. Maybe it was someone out of her past she had messed up. I mean the woman was a crazy obsessive. I'll take over your cases and let you go ahead. Maybe a fresh pair of eyes is what I need."

"There's a real nasty one just come in," said Simon. "A missing ten-year-old."

"Name?"

"Charlie Devon. Was supposed to get on the school bus but never did. Parents are frantic."

"When did this happen?"

"This afternoon. Mother doesn't want to wait for the police. Wants us to investigate as well."

"You pair seem to be working in tandem," said Agatha suspiciously.

"That way, we get results," said Toni, giving Agatha a hard look, which seemed to say, don't interfere in my life again.

"Which school?"

"St. George's, Church of England, on the Evesham Road."

"I'll get on it right away."

Agatha stopped her car before she got to the school because she could see a mobile police unit being set up in front of it.

She could hardly go into the school and start to interview people with the police around. Police would be at the parents' home as well.

She sat and scowled horribly in thought. The road shimmered in the heat in front of her.

Agatha felt suddenly helpless. The police would be scanning the CCTV cameras that festooned Mircester.

Think! she commanded herself.

Suppose the kid hadn't been snatched by some paedophile. The day was scorching. What would I have done at his age? What if he had a bad report card and wanted to put off the moment of going home?

Agatha drove round to the back of the school and pulled out an ordnance survey map and studied it closely.

Then she phoned Mrs. Freedman. After asking her secretary how she was, Agatha demanded, "Where would your little grandchildren go for a swim on a hot day near St. George's School on the Evesham Road?"

"My daughter's with me. Hang on a moment."

Agatha waited impatiently, listening to the faint murmur of voices at the other end of the line.

At last Mrs. Freedman came back on the line. "There is one place, Wikley Hole. It's a disused quarry filled with water. It's pretty dangerous and children are warned not to go there."

Agatha took out a notebook and pen and asked for directions.

Finally she rang off and drove in the direction of the quarry. She parked on a road near the quarry and set off in the heat. At last she stood on the lip of the quarry and looked down into the sinister black water. Nothing moved. She saw a sort of rabbit track leading precipitously down to the water.

Agatha hesitated. The heat was suffocating and she had a longing to return to her air-conditioned car, but something drove her on. She slithered down the track, getting her hands full of thorns as she had to grab on to various gorse bushes to stop herself from sliding.

At last she found herself on a grassy ledge beside the water. She was about to turn away when she heard a sob.

"Charlie," she said gently, "come out. I am a friend of your parents and I've come to take you home."

"C-can't," choked a little voice from the bushes next to her. "I ain't got no clothes. The big boys took 'em."

"All you've got to do is to come out and follow me up to my car. I won't peek. I've got a rug in the car you can cover yourself with."

"You won't look! Promise!"

"Cross my heart and hope to die. Just follow me."

Agatha set off slowly back up the track. She could hear the boy coming up behind her by the occasional sobs which racked his body. Once at the car, she fished a travel rug out the back and closed her eyes.

The rug was finally snatched from her,

and Charlie said, "You can look now, missus."

He was small for his age with a mop of red curls and a freckled face. At Agatha's urging, he got into the passenger seat.

Agatha took out the file on him with his parents' address, located it on the town map and set off.

"What happened?" she asked.

It all came pouring out. He was in trouble at school. He had cheeked the maths teacher, Miss Water, and had been told to take a letter to his parents. He had wanted to put off going home and so he had nipped out the back of the school. It was so hot he had decided to go for a swim. He had just got into the water when some boys came down. They snatched his clothes and ran off laughing.

"There's an ice-cream van," said Agatha, stopping. "Want one?"

"Yes, please. Chocolate."

While Agatha waited for a cone with two scoops of chocolate ice cream, she phoned the boy's parents and then the Associated Press with a message that private detective Agatha Raisin had found the missing boy and was returning him to his parents.

A much recovered Charlie thanked her for the ice cream and then asked cautiously,

"You ain't one of them weirdos, are you?"

"I am a private detective, Agatha Raisin."

"Gosh! Cool!"

Agatha drove very slowly and was relieved to see several members of the press outside Charlie's home. Bill would be furious with her, but the agency could do with publicity.

As Agatha and Charlie got out of the car, cameras clicked, the house door opened and Charlie's mother came flying down the path, tears of relief streaming down her face.

Agatha introduced herself and had the satisfaction of seeing reporters taking down Mrs. Devon's impassioned thanks. Once in the house, Agatha was grilled by the police, who almost seemed to think she had staged the whole thing.

When she got back to her cottage, Agatha felt weary and suddenly frightened. The unrelenting heat seemed to hold a brooding menace. Old houses like Agatha's thatched cottage seemed to come alive as they settled down for the night with creaks and rustles in the thatch. She found she was jumping at every sound.

She thought of Wyckhadden. She could almost see waves breaking on the shore and feel fresh sea breezes on her cheeks. Agatha made a sudden decision. One week-end away would not hurt.

She phoned Jimmy Jessop and told him she would drive down on the following day, Friday, and spend the week-end with him.

Jimmy was delighted. He said crime was quiet and he would be able to spend the whole week-end with her. Agatha then phoned Toni and told her she would be away for the week-end.

As soon as Agatha had rung off, Toni phoned Simon with the news. "It would be great if we had a break and solved the murders before she came back," said Toni.

Simon brightened at the prospect of spending the week-end with Toni. "I can tackle Jessica Fordyce on Saturday," he said. "Your photograph has been in too many newspapers. I'll pose as a fan. You can tackle some of the others. I'll book us two rooms in a bed and breakfast. There might be someone in the village who takes paying guests. I'll look it up."

Early the following morning, Agatha heaved a heavy suitcase into the boot of her small car. She had nervously packed clothes for every occasion. Doris picked up the cats, saying, "I'll water the garden for you while you're away. The poor flowers are dying in this dreadful heat."

Agatha had largely ignored the flowers. They reminded her too much of George and her own stupid folly in chasing after him.

She drove off under a glaring sun along roads where pools of silicon shone like lakes in the heat.

At last, by late afternoon, she topped a rise and saw beneath her the town of Wyckhadden, seeming to crouch before an endless flat sea.

Agatha had a good memory and remembered the road to Jimmy's bungalow. She recalled how vandals ripped up her mink coat. Jimmy had given it to his late wife, who had had it repaired. I wonder if he's got it, thought Agatha. I wouldn't mind having it back.

Jimmy had been watching for her and came out to meet her. "Let me," he said, taking her heavy case from her. He pecked her on the cheek. He still had a lugubrious face and large pale eyes under heavy lids. There were a few grey hairs in his black hair, but that was the only change Agatha could see in him.

He dumped Agatha's case in the hall. "Have you eaten?"

"Just stopped for a bacon sandwich on

the road."

"Then I'll take you out for dinner. There's a new place in town. Do you need to freshen up?"

"Yes."

"I'll show you where your room is, through here at the back. I'm proud of our guest room. My late wife had a bathroom en suite put in."

The double bed was covered in one of those slippery silk covers that Agatha loathed. It was bright pink, as were the curtains at the window. The bathroom boasted a pink bathmat and the toilet was covered in pink chenille. Agatha wondered if the late Mrs. Jessop had been a Barbara Cartland fan.

She decided to hang up her clothes later. She washed her face and reapplied her make-up.

When she joined Jimmy again, she said, "I haven't changed. I'm just too hungry."

"You'll do. It's not a dressy place."

Obviously, thought Agatha uneasily. Jimmy was wearing a tropical shirt over grey flannels and grey socks with brown sandals.

"Things haven't changed much since your last visit," said Jimmy as he drove competently into the centre of the town. "The sea wall is ugly and blots out the view of the beach, but it's better than being flooded. Here we are. The great thing about this place is that they have a large car park."

Agatha's heart sank. The restaurant was called Chicky Chicken. A large neon chicken reared up against the paling night sky.

They entered the restaurant. "I booked a table," said Jimmy. "This place is awfully popular."

There was no air-conditioning and Agatha could feel little rivulets of sweat running down her back as they were ushered into a booth with plastic seating. The menu was on a tablemat. Agatha gloomily surveyed the menu. There was every kind of chicken dish: roast chicken, barbecued chicken, southern fried, chicken in a basket and chicken wings.

"I could murder a nice cold drink," said Agatha.

"I'm afraid they haven't got a licence," said Jimmy, "but they do a very good fruit squash."

"Okay," said Agatha bleakly. "I'll have one of those and some roast chicken, maybe with roast potatoes."

"Just chips."

"Oh, well, go for it."

"My wife had her last meal out here," said Jimmy, "before she became too weak. It will always have a special place in my heart."

After Jimmy had given their order to an acned waiter, Agatha asked, "What kind of cancer did she have?"

"Cancer of the breast."

"But I thought they could do wonders these days."

"Poor Margaret. She was so proud of her hair."

Agatha blinked, remembering Mrs. Jessop's tightly permed curls.

"She refused chemo and tried every alternative you could think of."

I shouldn't have come, thought Agatha. But I'll need to stop being snobbish. I like chicken, but I would also have liked a drink. Oh, well, I may as well get something out of this trip.

"Your late wife did enjoy that fur coat of mine," she said. "Do you still have it?"

"Margaret loved it so much, she left instructions to be buried in it."

Oh, my mink, mourned Agatha. All those beautiful little vermin which were better on my back than depopulating the natural species of these islands.

"Wasn't that considered . . . well . . . a bit odd?"

"Not at all. Margaret was much respected. Now, tell me about these horrible murders."

"Well . . ." Agatha paused as their food arrived. "I'll eat something and then I'll tell you," she said.

Her first bite of chicken removed much of her appetite. Even though Agatha's palate was geared to junk food, she found the chicken dry and tasteless. She wondered if they had boiled it first for stock. She seized the bottle of ketchup on the table and doused it and put another helping on her chips.

"You'll ruin the taste," said Jimmy severely. "That chicken is free range."

With legs like this, the poor bird was probably jammed in a cage until it finally died a welcome and premature death, thought Agatha. She gloomily forced herself to eat some ketchup-doused bird and then began to talk about the murders. She finished by asking, "You have some experience of murderers. I've told you about my suspects. Who do you think it could be?"

Jimmy shook his head. "He seems to have been a serial philanderer. There could be other women in his past. Was he ever married?"

"Snakes and bastards. He told me he had been married once but said he didn't want to talk about it. Excuse me. I must powder my nose." Agatha headed for the ladies' toilet. She had not wanted to make a phone call about the case in the noise of the restaurant.

Ensconced in a stall in the toilet, Agatha took out her phone and dialled Janet Ilston's number. "It's Agatha here," she said urgently. "Your brother was married once. Who was she and how did the divorce come about?"

"It was twenty years ago. Her name was Trixie DuVane. She was a young model. All legs and no brain. George wouldn't talk about it. All he said was that it was an amicable divorce."

"Have you any sort of address for her?"

"I do as a matter of fact. She wrote me a letter of condolence. Hang on a minute."

Agatha waited impatiently.

A woman hammered on the door. "Are you going to be in there all day?" she shouted.

"I've got AIDS," yelled Agatha. "Leave me alone."

There came shocked exclamations and the shuffle of feet as the ladies' toilet hurriedly emptied. Idiots still think you can get it from lavatory seats, thought Agatha.

Janet came back on the line. "She's now Mrs. Tragent. Number twenty-two, River Lane, Jericho, Oxford."

Agatha thanked her and rang off. She hurried back to Jimmy.

"You look stressed. You should forget about the murders and enjoy the week-end," said Jimmy severely. "I mean, here we are together again." He leaned across the table, and taking Agatha's hand in his, gave it an affectionate squeeze.

A woman marched up to their table and glared at Agatha. She had dyed blond hair and a fake bake. "I waited outside the loo to see who it was. I wouldn't touch her if I were you," she said to Jimmy. "I heard her loud and clear. She's got AIDS."

"Sod off!" yelled Agatha, her face flaming.

"What's this about, Agatha?" asked Jimmy.

"I only went to the toilet to make a phone call, Jimmy. About the case. I thought you might think it rude that I was still working on the murder. She was hammering on the door. I only said I had AIDS to get rid of her."

Jimmy fished in his pocket, took out his warrant card and flashed it at the woman. "Police," he said. "Go away."

When the woman had retreated, he said, "How could you, Agatha? This is a small gossipy town and I have my reputation to consider."

"I didn't know they still lived in the dark

ages here," protested Agatha. "What if I did have AIDS? Think of the sheer cruelty."

"One would think your attitude to the poor people cursed with a dreadful illness is a bit callous."

"I am *not* callous. I just didn't think," said Agatha, near to tears. "I'd like to get out of here before they decide to stone me." Jimmy paid the bill and they left the restaurant. They walked in silence to the car.

"Let's go for a drink," said Agatha.

"I would rather go home, if you don't mind."

Agatha tried to think of something, anything, to say to lighten the atmosphere. But Jimmy's disapproval filled the car like a dark cloud.

Once in the bungalow, he said stiffly, "I would like an early night."

"Look, Jimmy, I . . ."

"Agatha, I am a respected member of the Rotary Club and a verger at the church. I am in line to be made superintendent. My reputation is precious. Please go to bed and leave me alone."

Agatha trailed off miserably to the spare room and sat on the bed. She had to admit to herself that she had nourished a dream of maybe marrying Jimmy and settling down. No more fears of being left alone in old age. No more frights and serpents. She felt ashamed of her remark about AIDS. She felt lonely.

She longed to phone Charles to come and rescue her, but that would be adding insult to injury as far as Jimmy was concerned. The room was stifling. Agatha wanted a cigarette. She looked around, but there was no ashtray in sight. She quietly left the room and made her way to the kitchen. Agatha could hear Jimmy leaving the bathroom and going to his own room.

The kitchen was intimidating in its housewifely cleanliness and décor. Gingham curtains hung from the windows. Appliances of every kind gleamed and glittered. There was a pot of geraniums on the table. Agatha felt one of the leaves. Fake! That cheered her up a bit.

She took a saucer down from a cupboard, sat down at the kitchen table and lit a cigarette. With a sigh of relief, she took a long drag on her cigarette and blew a smoke ring up to the ceiling. Too late, she saw the smoke alarm. It went off with a shrill sound.

The kitchen door was wrenched open and Jimmy, in striped pyjamas, glared at her. "No smoking, Agatha."

Agatha sighed and stubbed out the cigarette. Jimmy went out and slammed the door behind him.

Returning to her room, Agatha packed her suitcase. There was no point in staying on. But then it dawned on her that Jimmy had probably set a burglar alarm. She tiptoed quietly to the front door. There it was.

But beside it was the fuse box. She tiptoed back. She listened. Snores were coming from Jimmy's room. He can't be that upset, thought Agatha sourly.

Returning to her room, she scribbled out a note for Jimmy. "Something's come up. Got to go. Didn't want to wake you. Agatha," and left it on her pillow.

Quietly she lifted her suitcase and crept along to the front door. She reached up to the fuse box and cut the electricity, unlocked and unbolted the front door and went out to her car.

The moon was riding high above. She saw to her dismay that Jimmy's car was blocking her own.

But she felt she could not bear a night in his house. Agatha cautiously made her way back indoors. She followed the sound of snoring and crept into Jimmy's room. He was lying on his back, large snores reverberating round the room. The curtains were drawn back and Agatha could see his car keys on the bedside table. She picked them up.

Back outside, she moved Jimmy's car by releasing the handbrake and letting it slide down into the road. She loaded her suitcase into the boot of her own car. The night seemed to have brought no relief from the heat.

The clock on the dash said ten thirty. Agatha could hardly believe it was still so early. A lifetime seemed to have gone past since she had first arrived. She crept back into the house and left the car keys on the kitchen table.

She drove down to the Garden Hotel, where she had stayed before, booked into a smoking room and then made her way down to the bar, where a large gin and tonic soothed her rattled nerves.

Chapter Six

Simon, clutching an autograph book in which he had scrawled the forged signatures of various celebrities, rang the bell outside Jessica Fordyce's door. He still had hopes of getting close to Toni and wished she were with him.

A young man answered the door. He was barefooted and wearing only a pair of ragged jeans slung low on his hips. He had the face of a dissolute fawn shadowed by a mop of glossy black curls.

"I was hoping to get Miss Fordyce's autograph," said Simon.

"Give me your book and I'll see what I can do." He held out his hand.

"Is it possible I could have a minute with her? I'm such a fan."

"No, it isn't." The door began to close.

"Who is it?" called a female voice from behind him.

"Some fan wanting an autograph. I'll get

rid of him."

"Don't do that, Rex. Musn't be rude to the fans. Let him come in."

"She's through that door," said Rex, and walked off.

Simon walked into the kitchen. "I'm just making coffee," said Jessica. "Take a seat." Jessica helped herself to a mug of coffee and sat down opposite Simon in front of a laptop. "Just a moment," she said.

She was wearing a gingham blouse, brief denim shorts and wedge-heeled sandals. "Aha!" she said at last. "Here we have the Web site of the Agatha Raisin Detective Agency and here is a photograph of Agatha with her staff. And here's you."

"Doesn't stop me from being a fan," said Simon gamely. "I'd still like an autograph." He pushed the book across the table to her. She pushed it back.

"Let's stop the charade," she said. "You're detecting and for some reason I seem to be on the list of suspects." She smiled at him. Simon felt blinded by that smile.

"Now I've met you," he said, "it does seem silly. You're just too beautiful to murder anyone."

She rose from the table. "I think that deserves a coffee. Milk and sugar?"

"Yes, please." Simon admired her long

legs. All thoughts of Toni were forgotten. He could feel himself being pulled into Jessica's aura, and then began wondering who the young man was.

As if by telepathy, the young man appeared in the kitchen. "He still here?" he complained.

"Don't be a grump. Rex, this is Simon Black, a private detective. Simon, Rex Dangerfield acts the part of one of my lovers in the soap."

"Lucky Rex," said Simon fervently.

"You should only talk to the police," complained Rex. "You said that Raisin female was a pain in the fundament."

"Run along, darling, and see if you can learn your lines for once."

Rex went out, slamming the kitchen door behind him.

"Luvvies," sighed Jessica. "They all think they're Laurence Olivier. I wanted rid of him but he gets bags of fan mail. So, Simon, how can I help you?"

"George Marston had affairs with at least two women in this village, Joyce Hemingway and Harriet Glossop," said Simon. "Have you heard anything about them?"

"There's a Mrs. Arnold in Carsely, a vindictive gossip. But she swears she heard Joyce Hemingway one night screaming at

George that she would kill him."

"Did you tell the police that?"

Jessica shrugged. "Only heard it the other day and I'm too busy to want to make statements. Look, are you sure Agatha had nothing to do with it? The whole village knows she was crazy about George."

"Agatha wouldn't dream of so vicious a murder," said Simon. "Besides, I know she's terrified of snakes."

"In that case, try Joyce Hemingway, and good luck, too. Now *there's* someone with a vicious temper. And furthermore, she worked once at London Zoo."

"In the snake house?"

"No, as a secretary, I believe."

"Where does she get her money from?"

"Don't know. Ask her — and then duck! I must get on and take Rex through his lines."

"It's been lovely meeting you," gabbled Simon. "Perhaps I could see you again?"

"I'm very busy, but here's my card. Phone and ask."

Simon stood outside her cottage, feeling dazed. Could this be love? Or was he acting like a starstruck teenager?

He took out his phone and called Toni. "I'm in the pub," she said. "Fred Glossop chased me off, Mrs. Glossop was nice but unhelpful, and Joyce Hemingway isn't at home. How did you get on?"

"I could do with a drink. Wait there and I'll join you."

The sight of Toni, slim, fair-haired and beautiful, usually made Simon's heart lurch, but for the first time, all he could think about was Jessica.

Jimmy Jessop struggled awake. Someone was hammering at the front door. He struggled out of bed and went to answer it.

"Why, Joe!" he exclaimed, recognising a fellow Rotary Club member. "What's up?"

"I nearly ran into your car," said Joe. "Do you usually park it in the middle of the road?"

Jimmy looked past him. His precious BMW was slewed at an angle across the road. Then he saw that Agatha's car had gone.

"I'm sorry. I'll move it right away. I had a guest and she must have moved my car to get her own out."

Jimmy got his car keys and in striped pyjamas and tartan slippers shuffled out to move his precious vehicle. His face tightened as he realised Agatha had not even put the handbrake on.

He parked it again in his short drive and

hurried indoors to dress. On his way out, he noticed the burglar alarm was switched off and cursed Agatha under his breath. He drove straight to the Garden Hotel, guessing that Agatha had probably gone there, only to find out she had checked out.

Jimmy thought, almost tearfully, of his late wife, who had never caused him a moment's anxiety. Why on earth had he invited that hellcat back into his ordered life?

Toni listened impatiently as Simon went on and on about Jessica Fordyce, what she had said and how she had looked. No wonder I've got into trouble in the past with older men, thought Toni. Young men are so damned emotionally immature. Just listen to him burbling on.

At last she interrupted him with "Yes, all very well. The only interesting bit is about Joyce Hemingway. How are we going to get to her? I wish Agatha wasn't so keen on publicity. As Jessica found out, our photos are on the agency Web site."

"We could listen in on her," said Simon.

"How?"

"I bought a gadget. One of those listening devices. It's a through-the-wall one. It's got a special ceramic microphone. The unit can turn the surface of any wall into a microphone and let me hear conversations made on the other side of the wall. It can listen through thirty centimetres of concrete."

"I don't like it," said Toni. "It seems a dirty business, listening in on people in their homes."

"We're in a dirty business. If we don't get a break in this case, then Agatha might end up bitten to death by adders."

Toni hesitated. "Have we thought of everything? I mean, are we sure Fiona was the only one in Lower Sithby that might have wished to kill George? Yes, of course I know she didn't, but there might be another female we're missing."

"Yes, but we're in Carsely, so let's get on with it here," said Simon. "I thought we'd wait until after dark."

"Look, you do what you must, but I don't want to be part of it," said Toni. "I'm off to see Mrs. Bloxby. She knows most of what goes on in this village."

Simon watched her retreating back, and then shrugged. He would wait until it got dark and set up his listening device outside Joyce's cottage.

Agatha drove to George's ex-wife's home in Jericho in Oxford, parked and got out into the dusty heat. A parking sign said RESI-

DENTS ONLY. She hoped the meter men had finished their checking for the day.

Mrs. Trixie Tragent lived in a neat terraced house with a blue door. Agatha rang the bell. At first she thought the slim beauty facing her must be Trixie's daughter, until her sharp eyes recognised the signs of surgical lifting on the face and the silicone of the splendid breasts revealed by a low-cut green linen top. Masses of cleverly dyed blond hair tumbled down on her shoulders. Agatha wondered if she had hair extensions.

"Who are you and are you going to stare at me all day?" demanded Trixie.

Her voice was harsh.

"Sorry," said Agatha. "Here's my card. I'm investigating the death of your ex-husband."

"You'd better come in, although I've already spoken to one of your officers."

Agatha realised that Trixie had bad eyesight and had been unable to read her card, but had assumed she was from the police. She followed her into a small front room. Green linen blinds covered the windows. The walls were green and the three-piece suite was also covered in green linen. There was a large oil painting of Trixie over the fireplace, wearing a green dress.

"Like I already said to the police, I haven't seen George this age. Poor George. Never could keep it in his pants. That's why we broke up."

"Has your husband met him?"

"Rory? Naw. We're divorced. George came to our wedding, but that was fifteen years ago."

"Do you have any children by George?"

"Naw. He wanted brats but I said I wasn't going to spoil my figure."

"I wonder if he had any illegitimate children," said Agatha.

"Hardly likely."

"But all his affairs . . ."

"Usually went for old birds. He had one of those complexes. Some Greek. Forget. Well, the sun is over the poop deck or whatever. Fancy a drinkie?"

"Yes, please," said Agatha. "I'm driving but one wouldn't hurt."

"What'll it be?"

"Gin and tonic, if you've got it. May I smoke?"

"Sure, knock yourself out."

Agatha prowled around the room until she found a small glass ashtray on the mantelpiece.

Trixie came back in after a few minutes, carrying a tray with the drinks. Her eyes had changed from a muddy brown to bright green. Contact lenses, thought Agatha.

"It's a funny thing, though," said Trixie. "I just remembered. If there was one thing in this world that George was afraid of, it was snakes. He was posted somewhere — can't remember where — but he'd been bitten by some snake and rushed to hospital. He wrote me, saying he had nightmares about the beasts. Pretty awful if the murderer knew that."

Agatha took a strong gulp of her drink. The murder of George was becoming even more frightening. The sheer viciousness of it was practically beyond belief. She was tired after her long drive. The little room was hot and stuffy.

"Can I have one of your cancer sticks?" asked Trixie.

"Go ahead." Agatha offered her a packet of Bensons.

"I shouldn't really," said Trixie. "Have you noticed that women smokers get those nasty wrinkles on their upper lips?"

"No, I hadn't," lied Agatha, privately vowing again to try to give up the habit. "So you hadn't heard from George in a long time?"

"That's right. Apart from one odd message. Forgot all about it. I didn't ring him because I suppose I still feel nasty about the way he cheated on me."

"What did he say?"

"He sounded a bit drunk. He said something about needing a lawyer and could he have the name of my one who handled our divorce. I thought, the silly bugger's gone and got married again and got himself into trouble as usual."

I wonder if he married someone, thought Agatha with a rising feeling of excitement. Must check.

"You don't have a tape of the message?"

"I use the British Telecom answering service — you know, the one that deletes messages after thirty days. I didn't even save it for the thirty days but wiped it out. God, I hated George. Funny the effect he had."

Mrs. Bloxby told Toni that Sarah Freemantle's husband had arrived home. Toni would rather have tackled Sarah without the presence of her husband, but decided to try to see her anyway.

Sarah answered the door. "May I help you?"

"I'm from the Agatha Raisin Detective Agency," said Toni. "And . . ."

"I have nothing to say to you."

The door began to close.

A tall man loomed up behind Sarah. "Who is it?"

"Just someone selling something," said Sarah, and slammed the door.

Toni walked back to her car. It was the week-end, so Phil would be home. Perhaps he had heard something. She was just about to get into her car when the man she had glimpsed behind Sarah came hurrying out of the house. "Hey, you!" he called.

Toni waited. He came up to her. "What are you selling?"

"I'm not selling anything," said Toni. "I'm a detective, investigating the murder of George Marston."

He was a well-built middle-aged man with a deeply tanned round face, heavy eyebrows and a small pursed mouth. His eyes looked mean. "And what's that got to do with my wife?"

"I'm asking everyone that Marston worked for," said Toni.

"So why did Sarah say you were selling something? Are you trying to lie your way into houses?"

He was now standing very close to her, emanating threat.

Toni moved to one side. "You'll need to ask her. I told her who I was," she said.

"Get lost and don't come here again." He grabbed hold of one of her arms in a painful grip.

Toni looked at him steadily. "If you don't let go of my arm, I will call the police."

He reluctantly released her. Toni nipped into her little car and slammed the door.

When she told Phil Marshall about the encounter, he looked at her in dismay.

"It's just too bad of Agatha to send a young thing like you to investigate this murder. Someone dangerous is behind it. I'll phone her up and suggest I do any interviewing. You're too young to lose your life. Different for an old codger like me."

"Any gossip about Freemantle?"

"None that I've heard so far, but I'll ask about. What about a glass of lemonade?"

Simon thought Toni might have contacted him. He was bored waiting around for it to get dark. At last he set out for Jessica's cottage. He had come on his motorbike. The road sloped down to Jessica's cottage and so he switched off his lights and engine and cruised down, stopping short of the cottage, and dismounting in the shade of a sycamore tree. He took out his equipment, put on the headphones, and keeping to the shelter of cottages' garden hedges, made his way towards Jessica's cottage. He knew he should be listening in on Joyce Hemingway, but he longed to know what Jessica was saying.

Opposite Jessica's cottage was a field, bordered by trees. He slipped across the road into the shelter of the trees and pointed the machine at the cottage.

Nothing but absolute silence. Then he noticed there was no car outside. Either Jessica had gone back to London or was out for the evening.

Stubbornly, he decided to wait. A warm wind had got up and rustled in the leaves above his head. He arranged himself comfortably with his back to a tree. He had drunk a lot in the pub to pass the time, and his eyelids began to droop. Soon he was fast asleep.

He awoke suddenly, feeling something moving on his back. Simon jumped to his feet. Some creature, he guessed, must have fallen out of the tree and down his back. He stood and tore off his shirt just as whatever it was bit him painfully. A bright moon was shining down through the leaves and to his horror, he saw a small snake, slithering off.

Quickly, he hid his equipment behind a tree and raced off to Moreton-in-Marsh hospital. Outside the hospital, he phoned Toni.

"I've been bitten by a snake."

"What? Where?"

"Never mind that now. Go to the trees opposite Jessica's cottage. I've hidden my equipment behind one of the trees right opposite. Get it. I can't risk the police finding it on me."

He rang off. Toni had returned to Mircester several hours ago. She got in her car, and, as Simon was being raced in an ambulance from Moreton to Cheltenham General Hospital, Toni set out again for Carsely.

To her relief, Jessica's cottage was in darkness. She located the listening device and was just about to pack it into a carrier bag she had brought with her when she remembered that Sarah Freemantle's cottage was close by. Despite her previous scruples, Toni suddenly found the temptation irresistible. Keeping to the trees, she crept along to opposite Sarah's cottage and pointed the listening device at it and clamped on the earphones.

To her horror, she could hear Sarah sobbing. Then came her husband's voice. "You will tell me the truth if it takes all night."

"I d-didn't h-have an affair with him," sobbed Sarah. "L-Leave me alone, Guy."

"I'm going to heat up the hot plate and put your hand right down on it and you'll tell me."

"*No!*"

Toni took out her mobile and dialed 999. "Shots fired at ten, Blackberry Lane, home of Sarah Freemantle, Carsely," she shouted, disguising her voice as best she could.

Taking out a pencil torch, she flicked it at a small notebook and found Sarah's number. Mr. Freemantle answered.

"Police on the way, you murdering bastard," said Toni, and rang off. She ran to her car with Simon's equipment and roared off. She drove straight to the vicarage and thrust the carrier bag with Simon's equipment at a startled Mrs. Bloxby.

"Hide this, please," pleaded Toni. "I'll explain later."

She then drove back to Sarah's cottage and waited. The police might have recognised her voice on the phone so better to confront them and say she thought she heard screams and shots from the house.

Soon the sound of approaching sirens filled the air. Bill Wong was the first on the scene. "Armed response unit is on the way. Did you phone?"

"Yes," said Toni. "I was going to interview Mrs. Freemantle when I heard her scream something like, 'Don't burn me!' and then I thought I heard a shot."

Other police arrived on the scene. The

door of the cottage opened and Guy Freemantle came out.

"Down on the ground," yelled Bill. "Get down on the ground."

A helicopter landed in the field opposite and disgorged the armed response unit.

Guy looked suddenly terrified. He sank to the ground. Bill went forward and handcuffed him.

Armed police burst into the house first, followed by Bill and Alice Peterson.

Sarah was sitting on the floor of the kitchen, sobbing. She had a cut lip and a black eye. The hot plate on the cooker burned fiery red. "He was going to burn me," she whispered. "I think he's broken my ribs."

Alice phoned for an ambulance.

An hour later, Toni sat in an interviewing room at police headquarters. She had had plenty of time to rehearse her story. Wilkes began the interview.

Toni stuck to her story that she had been visiting Phil Marshall and had gone to see if she could get an interview with Sarah Freemantle. She said she was worried about her because she had been there earlier and had judged Guy Freemantle to be a violent man. She had heard screams and then she swore she thought she had heard shots.

She was taken through her story over and over again to see if it changed in the slightest.

Wilkes then said, "We had a report this evening from Cheltenham General that Simon Black was taken in there with a snakebite. Did you know about it?"

"Yes, he phoned me, but, as I said, I decided to see Sarah first before going to the hospital."

Wilkes shuffled some notes. "He says he was waiting under a tree opposite Jessica's Fordyce's cottage to see if she would return home because he wanted to ask her a few more questions. He said he fell asleep and woke when he felt something down the back of his shirt. Now, adders don't slither about in nighttime, nor do they drop out of trees. It is our belief that someone put it down his shirt deliberately."

"So where was Jessica Fordyce?" asked Toni.

"Dining at the Countryfare restaurant in Moreton, as several of her fans can testify."

"But surely that closes at nine thirty?" said Toni. "It must have been after dark when Simon got bitten."

"Why do you assume that?"

"Because it was dark when he called me,"

said Toni quickly.

"Your statement will be typed up and then I want you to sign it. We will probably want to talk to you again tomorrow."

Agatha Raisin struggled awake as the phone beside her bed rang shrilly. She listened in horror as Toni told her of the attack on Simon. "I'm on my way to the Cheltenham General," said Toni.

"I'll meet you at the hospital," said Agatha.

She hurriedly dressed, sharply aware of sinister rustlings in the thatched roof above her head. The thatch usually rustled at night, but now she imagined snakes slithering about.

Agatha found Toni waiting for her at the entrance to the hospital. "I should have stopped you from coming," said Toni. "He's asleep and doing all right. But I wanted to talk to you about Guy Freemantle."

She described the arrest of Guy but carefully omitted any mention of Simon's listening device.

"So he beat her up and then was about to burn her hand," said Agatha. "Now, there's someone vicious enough to have done the murders. I wonder if he knows anything about snakes. And was he away all the time?

Where was he supposed to be?"

"Phil told me he's a senior welding inspector on an oil rig in Scotland."

"That's odd. The wife gave me the idea he was working abroad. I wonder if there's any way he could have been lurking around the village. I suppose the police will be checking his movements."

"Do you think Sarah will divorce him?"

"She might not. She doesn't have an income. Of course, she'd get alimony. Maybe she's been a battered wife for too long to break away."

"I don't feel like the drive back to Mircester," said Toni. "I think I'll sleep in the car and see Simon first thing in the morning."

"Did Simon interview anyone else?"

"He saw Jessica Fordyce and from the look on his face I think he fell hook, line and sinker," said Toni. "But he was going back there to listen outside her cottage."

Agatha looked at her sharply. "These old cottages have thick walls. Where was Simon when the snake got down his shirt?"

"He was sitting under a tree opposite the house and fell asleep."

"Any car passing along that road would have seen him in the headlights. We'll need to find out if Sarah Freemantle's husband came home while Simon was asleep and if he knows anything about adders."

Agatha's bearlike eyes bored into Toni's face. "Wait a bit. Was Simon using a listening device?"

"N-no," stammered Toni, turning red.

"So he was! You're a bad liar. What if the police look through his stuff and find it?"

Toni hung her head. "I gave it to Mrs. Bloxby."

Agatha groaned. "Listening devices are illegal in Britain. We'd better get over to the vicarage first thing in the morning. If Alf Bloxby finds it, that pious pillock who doesn't like me a bit will probably take the stuff to the nearest policeman. Is that how you found out that Guy was abusing his wife?"

"I couldn't resist the temptation. I didn't know it was illegal. I protested about it to Simon because I thought it was sneaky."

"You'd better come home with me," said Agatha. "We'll call early at the vicarage in the morning and get the damn thing and then go and see Simon."

The next morning, the vicar padded about the sitting room, looking for his favourite pen. He could hear the clatter of dishes in the kitchen as his wife prepared breakfast.

Thinking he might have dropped it on the

floor, he got down on his hands and knees and looked under the sofa. He saw a small carrier bag he didn't recognise and pulled it out.

He was just about to open it when his wife walked in. "Leave that!" said Mrs. Bloxby quickly. "I'm keeping it for someone. Your breakfast's ready. What are you doing on the floor?"

"I've lost my pen. It's the gold-plated one I won in that crossword competition."

"It's on the mantelpiece, behind that vase."

The vicar got to his feet. "Oh, great."

"Now, have your breakfast."

When the vicar had collected his pen and gone into the kitchen, Mrs. Bloxby seized the bag and looked wildly around. She went through the French windows, down the garden and into the churchyard. Mrs. Bloxby had already examined the contents of the bag and had recognised the machine as a listening device, having recently read an article on spy gadgets. Mr. Barret-Jynes had been buried the day before. A spade was lying beside the freshly dug grave. She seized the spade, dug a hole, shoved the bag in, piled earth on top of it and then smoothed the earth flat with a hefty whack of the spade.

■ ■ ■ ■

After breakfast, the vicar decided to go out to the churchyard and say a prayer for the soul of Mr. Barret-Jynes. The day was fine, without the clammy heat of previous days.

He stood by the grave and bent his head.

A voice rose from the grave. "Alf Bloxby," said a deep voice. "You are arrogant."

He let out a gasp of fright, and, turning, ran back to the shelter of the vicarage.

"And that's wot I would like to say to 'im," said old Mr. Sither, walking past the churchyard.

"Me, too," said his friend Bert Camden.

"What's the matter?" cried Mrs. Bloxby. "Alf, you're as white as a sheet."

"I think I'm going mad," said the vicar. "I went to say a prayer at Mr. Barret-Jyne's grave and a voice from the grave spoke to me."

Oh, dear, thought his wife, that wretched gadget must still be switched on.

"What did it say?" she asked.

"Never mind," said the vicar quickly. "Do you think he's alive?"

"Poor Mr. Barret-Jynes had been lying dead for a week when he was discovered," said Mrs. Bloxby, forcing herself to remain calm. "Mrs. Carpie, who does for him, had been on holiday. She found him when she got back. She gave a terribly graphic description of the flies and smell. There is no way that man is alive. I'll go and look. It was probably some joker hiding behind a tombstone."

The vicar's face cleared and he looked fondly at his wife. How could any supernatural manifestation think him arrogant? "I'll go and have a look," he said.

"No, go and write your sermon. I'll do that."

Mrs. Bloxby hurried out to the churchyard. When she had banged the earth down flat, it must have triggered the machine.

She hurriedly dug it up again, opened the bag and switched the machine off.

She was just wondering where to hide it when she heard her husband calling her. She thrust the bag behind a nearby tombstone just as Alf appeared at the end of the garden.

"It's that Raisin creature," he called. "Did you see anyone?"

"No one at all."

Mrs. Bloxby hurried into the house to find Agatha and Toni waiting in the sitting room. The vicar had disappeared into his study.

"In the graveyard," said Mrs. Bloxby. "Come with me and get rid of the wretched thing. I'm surprised at you. Don't you know it's illegal?"

"I'll tell you all about it once I've got it," said Agatha.

They retrieved the bag and sat down together in the garden after Mrs. Bloxby had found a different bag to hide the gadget in case her husband appeared and recognised the original bag.

"So you see," said Agatha, after describing recent events, "Freemantle could have been on his way home and seen Simon in his headlights."

"But how would he recognise Simon?" asked Mrs. Bloxby.

"That's easy," said Toni. "Our photos are all on Agatha's Web site. It does make some investigations difficult."

Agatha's face turned pink. In her desire for publicity, she had somehow never thought that putting photographs of them all on the Internet might be a stupid idea. Her belief in herself, never very strong, took a plunge.

"We'd better see how Simon is getting on," she said. "We'll lock up this listening device in the office safe before we go to the hospital."

To Agatha's irritation, Simon seemed very cheerful. He said he had received a shot of antivenom and would probably be released from hospital on the following day.

His smile faded as Agatha gave him a blistering lecture on the folly of using an illegal listening device.

"Perhaps we should look around for some snake handlers," said Toni. "I mean an ordinary person can't know how to catch adders and how to handle them. And what about pet shops? Can anyone buy venomous snakes?"

Agatha opened her capacious handbag and took out her iPad. "Let me see." She typed busily. "Ah, here we are. You need to get a licence from the council. But you don't need to bother in Ireland. Wonder if any of our suspects have been to Ireland recently?"

"How do we find out?" asked Toni.

"I wish we had the resources of the police," said Agatha. "We'll just need to ask them."

"Perhaps we should widen the field," said Toni. "I mean, while we're concentrating on Glossop, Freemantle, Hemingway and

Fordyce, it could be someone else we don't know about. Marston was a serial shagger." Agatha winced. "There might be someone else with a reason to kill him. And I don't know why Jessica Fordyce is on the list. She's alibied up to her armpits. She's high profile. She could hardly walk into a pet shop and collect adders without being recognised. Anyway, I doubt very much if pet shops sell adders. People go for more exotic things, like boa constrictors."

"I agree with Toni," said Simon. "I mean you've only got to look at Jessica. She's so beautiful and warm-hearted and . . ."

"Oh, shut up!" snapped Agatha. "Look, right at this moment, we have a villain in Freemantle. Any man who could treat his wife that way has a vicious jealous temper."

"I've been thinking about that," said Toni. "It seems more like a woman's crime. Marston had a drink with someone and that is how he initially got drugged. I can't see him settling down for a friendly drink with Freemantle. I just remembered, Phil might have another suspect. I visited him yesterday. He said we've ignored Carsely's villainess, Matilda Fraser. You remember, she was arrested for having a cannabis farm three years ago. Her husband, Tim, was believed to be the main villain and she's got three young children, so she got a suspended sentence, but gossip has it that Tim, who cleared off and can't be found, was only dancing to her tune. She wore the pants in the house."

"So what's she got to do with George?"

"She evidently employed him to do her garden. It was a wreck after all the cannabis plants were taken away. She took down the greenhouse and wanted the rest turned into a conventional garden."

"Let's go and see her now," said Agatha.

"What do you want me to do when I get out of here?" asked Simon plaintively.

"There's a backlog of cases. Start work on some of them. Our clear-up rate is slipping."

Chapter Seven

Toni left her car parked in Mircester. Agatha drove them to Mircester Library to read up on Matilda Fraser. Her lawyer had pleaded eloquently on her behalf, saying she was a battered wife and that Tim Fraser had forced her into allowing the cannabis farm. When police had raided the property, Tim Fraser was missing. His wife said he must have had a tip-off. Police were still searching for him.

Carsely is getting more like things were when I lived in London, thought Agatha. People don't really know their neighbours as much as they used to.

Matilda lived in the old council estate on the edge of the village. Although it was still referred to as the council estate, most of the houses were now privately owned.

She lived in a house at the end of a cul-de-sac. Unlike the others, which were mainly terraced, it stood alone.

Matilda Fraser was a scrawny woman with dyed red hair. She was obviously an addict of the tanning parlour because her skin was an unhealthy orange-brown. She had pale hooded eyes and a thin drooping mouth.

"I don't need your card," she said. "I know who you are. What do you want?"

"I need your help," said Agatha. "I am investigating the murder of George Marston."

"Oh, that? You'd better come in."

The living room was dominated by a huge flat-screen television. In front of it slumped a young man with a shaved head. "This is my son Wayne. Get lost, Wayne."

Wayne shuffled off. Matilda clicked off the television. "Sit down," she ordered.

Agatha sat gingerly on the edge of a stained brown corduroy sofa. Toni sat beside her.

"Whaddayawantoknow?" asked Matilda, running all her words together.

"I wondered if George talked to you about anyone he was afraid of?"

"No. We did have a laugh, though. Always joking and laughing, that was my George."

"Your George?" Agatha's eyes sharpened. "Were you close?" Not her, surely, thought Agatha. The woman hasn't even got her own teeth!

"Bit of a kiss and a cuddle," said Matilda complacently. "But that's fellows for you. Had to fight 'em off all my life."

My self-worth is lower than whale shit, thought Agatha bitterly. All the trouble and expense I went to to try to lure him.

"Did he say anything about snakes?" asked Agatha. "I believe he had a phobia about them."

"Didn't say nothing to me. I found one of the bastards in my garden the other week. Took its head off with the spade. Nasty, crawly things."

"Did you tell the police?"

"Had enough o' them. Anyway, a garden's always crawling with nasties. Like to see it?"

"Just have a look," said Agatha.

The garden had obviously been neglected since the death of George and was in need of watering. Flowers hung limply in the hot still air.

"That's odd," said Toni.

"What's odd?" demanded Matilda.

"That rockery in the middle of the lawn. I mean, it spoils the look of the garden. And half the plants are dead."

"If you've had enough of poking around," said Matilda harshly, "you'd better go. I got things to do."

▪ ▪ ▪ ▪

As they got in Agatha's car, Agatha could feel excitement emanating from Toni. "What's up?" she asked.

"That rockery is all wrong," said Toni. "George Marston, by all accounts, was an expert gardener. He would never have allowed a thing like that."

"So she's got bad taste. So what?"

"No one ever found the missing Tim Fraser. With him out of the way, Matilda could claim to be a bullied wife, not responsible for the cannabis farm."

"Now there's a flight of fancy," commented Agatha. "How are you going to prove it?"

"She got upset when I asked about the rockery. If Tim is under there, then she'll think about moving him. I'll stake the place out after dark."

Agatha felt tired and demoralised. But if there was a faint chance that Toni was right, she did not want to be upstaged by her beautiful sidekick.

"Let's drive up round the back," said Agatha. "I noticed the back garden bordered onto a field. We could wait there."

Toni repressed a sigh. It had been her

idea. Probably nothing in it. But if it came off, she did not relish the idea of Agatha muscling in.

As they settled down that evening at the edge of a field bordering the back of Matilda's garden, Agatha found herself thinking about Simon's listening device. It was awfully tempting. But, she decided firmly, it must not be used. It was illegal, and the thought that, were it not, anyone could easily spy on their neighbours.

The air was close and sticky. Agatha felt hot because she was wearing high boots as a protection against any possible lurking adders. Toni was sitting on the grass at the edge of the field. Agatha was weary. She was tired of standing.

"Aren't you frightened of being bitten?" she whispered crossly.

"By adders? No, not at this time of night. Besides, standing up there, you must be silhouetted against the moon."

Agatha sat down quickly.

"Where's Charles these days?" muttered Toni.

"I don't know. I haven't tried to phone. You know Charles, he comes and goes."

"And James?"

"Somewhere on his travels."

Toni clutched Agatha's arm. "Shh! A light's gone on in the kitchen at the back. We should try to get nearer."

"We're near enough to hear any digging," whispered Agatha. "It's so quiet. Any movement and she might hear us."

"What! The whole bleeding thing?" came a masculine voice.

"I think that's Wayne, the son," said Toni.

There came the sounds of digging. Then Wayne's voice. "I've loaded up the first wheelbarrow lot. Where are we going to put the stuff?"

"Take it through the gate at the end of the garden," ordered Matilda.

"The farmer'll find it."

"He's letting that field lie fallow. He won't notice."

"Let's get out of here," said Agatha hurriedly. "I'll phone Bill."

Once they were both back in Agatha's cottage, Agatha phoned Bill's mobile phone number, hoping he would answer it before his mother rushed into his bedroom and got hold of his phone.

When his sleepy voice came on the line, Agatha began to talk urgently.

"We haven't got a search warrant," said Bill, "and we won't be able to get one until tomorrow."

"Lie," urged Agatha. "Say we think Tim Fraser is there. Don't say we think he's under the rockery or they won't bother. He's a fugitive. You don't need a search warrant."

"I'll see what I can do," said Bill, and rang off.

"We'll wait outside the estate," said Agatha, "and when the police arrive, we'll follow them up to the house."

Agatha fretted that the police were not going to come until, up on the hill above Carsely, she saw the first flickering blue light of a police car.

"The cavalry's arrived," she said. "Keep your fingers crossed."

"I really hope there isn't going to be another dead body. If there is, the village is going to be swamped by the world's press."

Three police cars drove up. Agatha followed them. The advance guard rang the doorbell, while another four policemen went round the back of the house. Then a policeman took a battering ram and crashed open the door.

As Agatha and Toni stood outside the house, an unmarked car bearing Bill and Wilkes arrived, Wilkes looking rumpled and bad tempered.

Wilkes glared at Agatha. "This had better not be a wild goose chase."

He and Bill walked up to Matilda's house and entered.

Agatha could hear shouts and then she heard Matilda scream.

Then a long silence.

People began to emerge from their houses. Matilda's home was taped off and Agatha and Toni were curtly ordered back behind the tape.

Forensics arrived and a photographer.

"No pathologist," said Toni.

Agatha could feel her ankles beginning to swell inside her boots and wished she had changed into sandals.

Just when she was beginning to contemplate a retreat to her car, Wilkes and Bill emerged. Behind them came policemen escorting three people in handcuffs: Wayne, Matilda and a tall, thin man. "Tell them, Dad, we didn't do nothing," said Wayne.

"That must be the missing Tim. Rats!" said Agatha.

"Cheer up," said Toni. "The police must have found something sinister or they wouldn't be arresting all of them."

Agatha ducked under the police tape and approached Wilkes. "What have you found?"

she asked.

"Follow us to Mircester," said Wilkes curtly. "You'll need to make a statement."

"But . . ."

"Just do as you're told for once in your life, Mrs. Raisin," snapped Wilkes. "Now, if you don't mind, I'd like to get to my car."

More police emerged from Matilda's house, carrying a large metal box.

"Let's go, Toni," said Agatha, returning to join her young detective. "We've got to go to police headquarters."

I'm sick and tired of being questioned, thought Agatha while she waited in the reception of police headquarters for Toni to emerge. She had not been able to claim that the idea that something was hidden in the rockery was her own, much as she had wanted to, because she knew Toni was being interviewed separately.

She took a little mirror out of her handbag and scrutinised her face. Any make-up she had put on earlier seemed to have melted in the heat.

Toni emerged, looking young and fresh and beautiful. "Did they tell you anything?" asked Agatha.

"Not really, not about what they had found, but at the end of the interview, a Detective Sergeant Briggs said, 'Thank goodness these murders have been solved.'

"I said, 'Do you mean the Frasers did it?' and he clammed up. They kept taking me over and over the reason I had guessed there was something odd about that rockery, so much I began to feel guilty."

"I'm about to burst with curiosity," said Agatha. "I'm going straight to Bill's home and I'm going to lurk outside until he gets back and demand an explanation. You can go home."

"No, I can't," protested Toni. "The whole thing was my idea, remember?"

"If you must," said Agatha sourly.

Bill recognised Agatha's car as he drove up the next morning. Agatha and Toni were asleep and he was tempted to escape into his home, but he knew that when Agatha woke up, she would come hammering on the door and upset his mother.

He went and rapped on the window. Agatha awoke immediately and slid down the window. "What's happened?"

"I shouldn't be talking to you," said Bill. "I don't want you in the house so let's go somewhere for a coffee. There's a Little Chef on the bypass."

"I know the one," said Agatha. "Wake up, Toni!"

When they were seated over coffees, Bill asked Agatha, "Are you up to hearing all this now? You're looking a bit haggard."

Agatha's hands fluttered protectively up to her face, an oddly childlike gesture that made Toni say quickly, "She's fine. Out with it."

"No dead body under that rockery," said Bill, "but a large metal box stuffed with money. Matilda claimed her husband had run off with the earnings they made from selling cannabis. But under the money were several books on adders: their habitats and how to handle them."

"And what have the Frasers to say about that?"

"Matilda claims that, yes, they hid the money while Tim cleared off to Scotland but she and her husband and Wayne swear blind that they know nothing about the books. Get this. They say someone must have put them there. Matilda says that she and Wayne recently went up to Scotland to see Tim, who was hiding out in Glasgow, and told him it might be safe to come back home for a bit, provided he kept out of sight."

"Wait a minute," said Toni, "where are their other three children? And where's the eldest, Wayne?"

"In care. Social took them away when Matilda went on trial. She didn't fight to get them back, either. We interviewed the three separately. Matilda said when she returned from Scotland, half the plants in the rockery were dead or dying. She put it down to the heat. Now, she says, someone must have dug it up, found the box, put the books in and built the rockery up again. There's something else. We found it out when we first arrested her and were looking into their backgrounds. As a young man, Tim Fraser drifted from job to job and one of his jobs was on a snake farm in Southend."

Agatha clutched her temples. "I don't get this. Why kill George?"

"He was her gardener. He might have come across it when he was doing the garden. They may have buried the box there before the idea of the rockery."

"But what about Fiona Morton and the snakes sent to me? What about the adder dropped down Simon's back?"

"Maybe they feared George had told Fiona about the box."

"And Simon?"

"Just a coincidental accident. He must have lain on an adder when he went to sleep."

"No, no, I can't believe it," said Agatha. "I think the Frasers are petty criminals. Both murders were vicious. The type prompted by jealousy. I don't believe the Frasers had anything to do with it. And what about Jessica Fordyce? Where was she when Simon was attacked?"

"She left for London earlier that evening. Look, Agatha. Case closed. Wilkes is making a statement to the press this morning. Now, I'm going to get some much-needed sleep."

When they had driven Bill home, Agatha said, "Do you think the Frasers did the murders?"

"I can't really believe it," said Toni. "I think Wilkes is being too premature. A defence lawyer can rip holes in the case. Unless their fingerprints were on the snake books, the rest is all just supposition."

"But the prosecutor can build up something. Tim Fraser did work, however briefly, on a snake farm. The books were hidden in their garden along with the profits from their illegal cannabis farm. I think if they wanted George out of the way, they'd simply have struck him down with a hammer or something. I don't believe they have it in them to plan the elaborate murder of George."

"Do you think George's sister, Janet, will consider the case closed?" asked Toni.

"I'm going to the office. I'll phone her from there."

But when Agatha phoned Janet Ilston, it was to find that Wilkes had already phoned her of the arrest. She listened to Agatha's doubts, and then said crisply, "It is my opinion that the police solved the murder of my poor brother and not you. I am terminating my contract."

"And that's that," said Agatha gloomily when Janet had rung off. "Can't afford to work for nothing in the middle of a recession. Let's start clearing up some of the other cases."

Agatha watched Wilkes on television that evening. She had hoped he might say the police were holding three people for further enquiries, but Wilkes said clearly that Timothy Fraser, his wife, Matilda, and his son Wayne had been charged with murder.

The doorbell rang. Agatha opened the door and found Charles standing there.

"Come in," she said glumly.

"What's up?" asked Charles. "I thought

you would be pleased the whole thing was over."

"Pour yourself a drink, sit down, and I'll tell you about it."

Charles listened carefully. When Agatha had finished, he said, "I don't see that you have a case, Agatha. It's too far-fetched to suggest that some mysterious killer decided to frame them by burying the snake books in their stash. Why would someone ever imagine that the police would look there?"

"Maybe it was a sort of insurance," said Agatha stubbornly. "Maybe whoever thought that if there was any sign the police were getting close, then an anonymous call would tip the police off. And what about the snakes sent to me? I wasn't anywhere near the Frasers."

"But surely it was all round the village that you were detecting. Maybe the Frasers just wanted you out of the way."

"Anyway," said Agatha, "what have you been doing with yourself?"

"Thinking of getting married."

"You! Who to?"

"Petronella Harvey-Booth."

"Who's she?" asked Agatha jealously.

"Young, pretty and rich. If she says yes I'll consider myself a very lucky man."

"Got a photo?"

Charles fished out his wallet and took out a photograph. "You must admit, Pet's quite attractive."

"You call her Pet?"

"Well, Petronella's quite a mouthful."

The photograph showed a tall, slim girl with long brown hair, a long face, long nose and a small mouth.

"And what has Gustav to say to your proposed marriage?"

Gustav was Charles's valet-cum-butler. "He thinks it's highly suitable."

"At least I won't have you dropping in here unexpectedly," said Agatha.

Charles smiled. "Will you miss me?"

Like hell, thought Agatha, feeling bereft.

"I'll get used to it," she said airily.

"About these murders, have you talked to Mrs. Bloxby lately?"

"Why?"

"Some little thing might have been happening in this village. What about Mr. Freemantle, for example? A wife beater, and he might have dropped that adder down Simon's neck. Let's go and visit her anyway."

"Don't you want to rush back to Pet?" asked Agatha.

"She's visiting her family in Devon at the moment."

"If she lives in Devon, how did you meet her?"

"She was staying with friends in Warwickshire. I met her at a party. I felt as though I had known her for ages."

Nobody wants me, thought Agatha. Men want frumpy women or girls who look like stick insects. I bet Pet's got hair extensions. I hope she has. People are warning against them, saying they cause baldness.

"I suppose we'd better call at the vicarage and find out if Mrs. Bloxby has heard anything."

The vicar answered the door to them, and, to Agatha's amazement, gave her a warm welcome.

"Come in, Mrs. Raisin," he said with a beaming smile. "It's always a pleasure to see you."

Agatha was not to know that the vicar was plagued with memories of that voice calling him arrogant. He had even preached a sermon on Sunday warning against the dangers of false pride. He could not quite believe his wife's explanation that someone was probably hiding behind a tombstone. The voice had seemed to come up from the grave.

Mrs. Bloxby met them in the sitting room

and suggested they should sit in the garden while her husband went off to his study.

"We were wondering whether you had heard anything," said Agatha. "I mean, perhaps one of the Freemantles' neighbours saw Simon under that tree."

"I haven't heard anything," said Mrs. Bloxby, "except that Fred Glossop has left again."

"I wonder why he came back," said Agatha. "They are separated, aren't they?"

"I believe Mrs. Glossop was frightened by the murders and sent for him."

"Where does he work?"

"He's a computer engineer, working for some Oxfordshire firm."

"Why did they never get a divorce?"

"According to the village gossip, it was an amicable separation."

"I don't believe in amicable separations," said Charles cynically.

"Perhaps I'll go and see her," said Agatha. "She might feel like talking a bit more without Fred around."

There was a notable change in Harriet Glossop's appearance. Her face was pale and she had lost weight. "Oh, it's you," she said in a flat voice. "And who is this man?"

"This is Sir Charles Fraith," said Agatha,

hoping to impress with Charles's title.

"I suppose you'd better come in. We'll sit in the garden."

"Your flowers could do with watering," commented Charles. Withered petals lay on the brown lawn.

"I've lost interest," said Harriet. "It's too hot. George was cheap compared to the prices gardeners around here are charging."

"We wondered if you could help us with something," said Agatha. "My colleague Simon Black was sitting outside Jessica Fordyce's cottage under a tree when he was attacked. Did you see or hear anything? A car driving along the road? Anything like that?"

"No. Look I don't know anything and what's more I don't want to know anything. I heard on the radio that those awful Frasers have been arrested, so why are you still poking around?"

"Because I can't quite believe they did it," said Agatha.

"And you know better than the whole police force?"

"I have this intuition . . ."

"Spare me," snapped Harriet. "There's a woman in Mircester who reads tarot cards. Why don't you try her? You should both be on the same wavelength."

"If you're determined not to help . . ." began Agatha.

"Look, I don't know a thing and I wish you'd just leave . . . now!"

They had walked to Sarah's cottage. As they strolled along the road, Joyce Hemingway came towards them.

"If it isn't the great detective," she sneered. "Trumped by the police."

"It was me who suggested there was something fishy about the rockery in their garden," said Agatha.

"Anyway, the police have closed the murder cases," said Joyce.

"I don't believe they did it," said Agatha. "And I've just found out something that might blow the whole case open again."

"What!" demanded Joyce shrilly.

Agatha smiled. "Now, wouldn't you just like to know. You were overheard threatening George, for starters. Come along, Charles."

"What on earth made you say that?" said Charles when they were out of earshot.

"I just felt like stirring the pond and seeing what rises out of the muck. I haven't the resources of the police, so I usually just blunder about until something breaks."

"Let's hope it isn't you," said Charles.

■ ■ ■ ■

James Lacey had just returned from his travels the next morning and was unpacking his suitcase when his doorbell rang.

He wondered whether to answer it. Newcomers to the village quickly found out he was an eligible man and since a good few of the newcomers were either divorcees or widows, some of them kept calling around with offers of cakes and jam when they knew he was at home.

Then he thought it might be Agatha. He had followed the murders in the newspapers and was anxious to hear what she thought about the arrest of the Frasers.

He left his bedroom, went downstairs and opened the door. A tall thin woman stood there. She held out her hand. "I am Petronella Harvey-Booth."

"I don't know you," said James impatiently.

"Of course you don't. I am shortly to become engaged to Charles Fraith."

"You'd better come in," said James, suddenly curious.

She perched herself on the edge of James's well-worn sofa. Not much of a looker, thought James. James thought she looked like a face in a mediaeval canvas, with her long nose and long straight hair and small mouth. Knowing Charles's liking for money, she must be very rich.

"So what's your engagement got to do with me?" asked James.

"I want to know why he spends so much time with your ex-wife. You see, Daddy told me to always be careful because we have a lot of money. So he hired a private detective."

James grinned. "There's a turn-up for the book. Agatha being stalked by a private detective."

"It seems Charles often spends the night at her cottage and he sometimes just lets himself in. I don't want to marry a man who has a mistress."

"I can assure you, they are just friends. Let's go next door and see if they are there. It will reassure you once you've met Agatha."

Agatha had just returned with Charles. She answered the door. "Oh, James, you're back," she said. "Who is this? Oh, I know. Charles showed me a photograph of you. Please come in. Charles is in the garden."

Charles rose to his feet and stared in surprise at Petronella. "Why, Pet! What are you doing here? Do sit down."

"I came to find out what you were doing here," said Pet, sitting on the edge of a garden chair and clutching a capacious handbag on her lap.

"Agatha's an old friend."

"I can see the old bit," said Pet waspishly. "It's the friendship I'm talking about."

"Bitch, bitch, bitch," muttered Agatha.

"You stay overnight with her," said Pet. "When you told her you were going to marry me, you described me as rich and then went on to ask if she would miss you."

There was a shocked silence. Charles found his voice first.

"That was a private conversation I had with Agatha just a short time ago."

Agatha suddenly snatched Pet's handbag, opened it and dumped the contents on the garden table, shoving Pet away as Pet tried to stop her.

Inside, she recognised a listening device like the one Simon had.

"You've been spying on me," howled Agatha. "This listening device is illegal and I am going to call the police."

She took her mobile phone out of her pocket.

"Don't," said Charles. "I want an explanation."

Pet burst into tears. James said, "I may as well tell you. Evidently Pet's papa has employed a private detective. He no doubt supplied Pet with the listening device. Anyway, that's what she told me before I brought her here."

"Daddy said I had to be careful," said Pet. "He said you might just be after me for my money. Please don't call the police."

"What agency?" demanded Agatha.

"Timmons."

Timmons was a new agency and Agatha had recently lost a couple of clients to them.

"I could do without the scandal," said Charles quietly.

"It's getting late," said Agatha. "Leave the listening device with me and I'll go and see them tomorrow. If you do not want me to go to the police, Miss Harvey-Booth, then I want a signed statement from you about how your father hired the agency and how they gave you the listening device. I also want the name of the detective assigned to your case."

"I c-can't."

"If you don't, I shall phone the police and then the newspapers," said Agatha.

"Charles!" wailed Pet.

"Sorry," he said. "I suggest you do just what Agatha says. Then you can go home and tell that father of yours that I am definitely not going to marry you."

"You're all horrid!" shouted Pet.

"Not as horrid as you," said Agatha.

As Agatha made her way to the Timmons detective agency in Mircester the following morning, she worried about Charles. He usually didn't betray any emotion at all, but he had been unnaturally quiet, saying only after Pet had signed the statement and left that he wanted to go home.

James had left as well to do his unpacking, after Agatha had asked him if he would like to come to Timmons with her in the morning. James had replied that he found the whole situation disgusting and that he had work to do.

A cool blond receptionist told Agatha to wait and Mr. Timmons would see her shortly. Agatha looked sourly around the reception area of her rival as she sank down into a black leather sofa. Glossy magazines decorated the coffee table in front of her. Abstract paintings hung on the cream walls.

Her own agency consisted of one large room with a secretary, Mrs. Freedman, at a desk by the window. Clients just walked in. Simon, Toni, Phil and Patrick as well as herself all had separate desks. No pictures decorated the walls, only press cuttings of the agency's successes. I never ever thought of remodelling it, thought Agatha. It's like my kitchen. No fashionable granite surfaces or copper pans, just the same white-painted cupboards that had been there when she bought the cottage. One square wooden table with four upright chairs surrounding it dominated the middle of the kitchen.

The door to the inner office opened and a large florid man breezed through. "If it isn't the famous Mrs. Raisin," he cried.

He had a large pear-shaped face and a double-breasted suit draped around his body. He wore rimless glasses behind which a pair of shrewd brown eyes, surveying her warily, belied the smile on his mouth.

"What can we do for you?"

Agatha opened a carrier bag and took out the listening device and put it on the table. "This is yours. It was used to illegally listen in on my conversations."

"Nonsense!"

"I have a sworn statement from Miss Harvey-Booth that her father hired you to spy on me. She was using this device herself."

"Silly cow!" Mr. Timmons took out a handkerchief and mopped his face.

"Before I go to the police, have you

anything to say?"

"My dear lady, I am sure we can come to an arrangement."

"Bribery as well?"

"No, no. The detective will be fired immediately. I knew nothing of this."

"When it comes to court," said Agatha, "I am sure he will say otherwise."

Mr. Timmons barked at the receptionist. "Get Baker in here!"

He turned to Agatha. "I am going to fire him in front of you."

A middle-aged man walked in. He was tall, dressed in a plain dark suit. Agatha thought he had ex-copper written all over him.

"This is Mrs. Agatha Raisin," said Timmons. "You have been using an illegal listening device and you're fired."

"It's this office's property," said Baker in a calm, deep voice. "I was using it on your instructions."

Baker gave his employer a long, hard look. Then he fished a powerful little tape recorder out of his pocket and switched it on. He plugged in an earpiece and listened, and then said, "Here it is." He unplugged the earpiece and amplified the sound.

Mr. Timmons's recorded voice suddenly sounded in the room. "Look, Baker, we've got an easy one here. This posh geezer, Colonel Harvey-Booth, has a daughter, Petronella, who wants to marry Sir Charles Fraith and wants the low-down on him. Get the listening device and get what you can."

"There's more," said Baker, searching the tape recorder again. Then his own voice saying: "Our client's daughter, Petronella, wants to have a go with the listening device herself. I told her that this Sir Charles Fraith had been spending time at Agatha Raisin's cottage and might be getting his leg over, and she wants to play detective herself." This was followed by Timmons's recorded voice: "Then let her have it. Raisin is a formidable rival and if we can upset her, all to the good. Petronella's dad is paying over the odds and if she wants to do the work herself, let her."

Baker switched off the recorder. "You may go," said Timmons.

Then he turned to Agatha, and said bleakly, "Is there any way I can stop you from going to the police?"

"Only one way. You close down here and move to another town."

"I can't do that!"

"Either that or I go to the police. You've got two weeks to shut down your operation here. I will come back at the end of two weeks. If you are still here, then I am really going to go to the police."

He got to his feet and Agatha stood up as well. He loomed over her. "I'll get even with you one day, see if I don't."

Agatha's handbag was open. She took out a small tape recorder, just like the one Baker had used.

"I have now taped that threat of yours. Dear me, you're not much of a detective, are you?"

Agatha popped the tape recorder back into her handbag and zipped it up.

"Bye," she said cheerfully.

Timmons stood rigid, his hands clenched into fists as he watched her go.

Agatha went to the office. She was suddenly weary of trying to find out who had murdered George. There was other work to be done.

Mrs. Freedman said everyone was out on other jobs and handed Agatha a list.

"Fine," said Agatha, scanning it, "except for Simon. Is he still in hospital?"

"No, he's out. He phoned in. He said he was going back to Carsely to see if he could find out who put that snake down his back."

"Snakes and bastards!" howled Agatha. "He'll get himself killed. Wasn't one attempt on his life enough for him?"

"It can't really be described as an attempt on his life," said Mrs. Freedman pedantically. "I mean, anyone bitten knows to go straight to hospital."

"I'm going over to Carsely to get him out of there," said Agatha.

"Don't you think you might be at risk yourself?"

"It's different. I can't avoid the place. I live there."

"Come to think of it," said Mrs. Freedman, "he should be all right. I mean, the case is closed, isn't it?"

The slamming of the office door was her only answer.

Simon had hoped to find Jessica at home. He had dreamt of her since that first meeting. Although he had never previously watched any of the soaps, he had bought a boxed set of *Emergency Tonight*, the series in which Jessica starred. But Jessica was not at home.

He stood outside her house, irresolute, wondering what to do. He knew she only visited the cottage at week-ends, but he had hoped against hope that she might have made a flying visit.

Simon knew he was supposed to be out

around Mircester looking for a missing cat, Agatha having again given him the bread-and-butter jobs of the agency. Before he had gone to Carsely, he had checked at the Mircester Animal Rescue Centre, hoping to find the cat easily. It was a Siamese. But no Siamese cat at all had been handed in.

The day was still and warm. There was a hosepipe ban and flowers in the cottage gardens drooped in the heat.

He knew Agatha was disappointed in him. Even before the snake attack, he had been outclassed by Toni. He now wondered what he had ever seen in her. Her blond beauty faded before Jessica's vibrant loveliness. Such was his obsession, that he found himself reluctant to leave Carsely.

He decided to go to the pub for a cold beer and was just heading in that direction when he looked up the hill and recognised Agatha's car speeding down towards the village.

Simon drove off out of the village by the alternative route and went back to Mircester. He parked in the main square, took out a photo of the missing cat and gloomily surveyed it. Then he had a bright idea. Surely one Siamese cat looked just like another. Simon came from a wealthy family and was never short of funds. He let in the clutch and drove to the nearest pet shop. Yes, they had a fine Siamese. "The one in your photo is a lilac point," said the salesman, "and I have one just like it."

"How much?" asked Simon.

"It's one of the rarer breeds. The cost is four hundred pounds."

Simon hesitated only a moment. "I'll take it," he said. He had a cat box in the car, which he kept for recovering lost cats. He went out of the shop and got it, paid with his credit card, and set off for the residence of a Mrs. Finney who had asked them to find the missing animal.

Agatha arrived back in her office, hot and cross. Toni was typing up a report at her computer. "Drop what you're doing," said Agatha, "and get down to Animal Rescue and see if anyone's handed in a Siamese cat."

"Isn't Simon on that one?"

"For some reason he went back to Carsely but I couldn't find him. Mrs. Finney keeps phoning." Agatha searched through the filing cabinet. "She gave us a lot of photos. Here's one. And ask if Simon even visited the rescue centre."

At the rescue centre, Toni was told she was in luck. A lilac point Siamese cat had just been handed in. Toni put the cat in a cat carrier and headed off for Mrs. Finney's home.

The first sound that met Toni's ears as Mrs. Finney opened the door was the unmistakable wail of a Siamese.

"We've found your cat," said Toni.

"But your colleague has just been here to give me back my cat," exclaimed Mrs. Finney.

"So this is not your cat?"

Mrs. Finney peered into the cat box. "How odd. She looks just like Bung Ho."

"Bung Ho?"

"A joke of my husband's and the name stuck."

"And you're sure you've got the right cat?"

"I know. I got Bung Ho microchipped. Come in and I'll check."

Once inside, Mrs. Finney prodded round the neck of the cat Simon had given her. "That's odd," she said. "No microchip. Let's have a look at the one you've got. Where did you find it?"

"Someone handed it in to the Animal Rescue Centre."

Mrs. Finney tenderly lifted out the cat that Toni had brought. "This one has a microchip," she said. "Oh, and here's one little black dot behind the left ear. Good heavens! This is Bung Ho. What do I do with the other one?"

"Do you mind keeping it for the moment?" asked Toni. "I've got to check where it came from."

She stood outside the house, thinking hard. Simon had money and Simon detested being demoted to looking for lost animals. Toni drove to the pet shop in Mircester.

Before going into the shop, she flicked through her camera until she found a group photo of the detective agency's staff. Then she went in. She showed the salesman the photograph, pointing to Simon. "Did he come in here recently and buy a cat?" she asked.

"Oh, yes. He bought a lilac point. Lovely beast."

"Thank you. That's all I want to know."

"Is anything wrong?"

"Nothing at all," said Toni.

She drove back to Mrs. Finney's home. "I wonder if you would mind keeping the extra cat," she said. "Animal Rescue really likes to find good homes for their animals."

"I'd love to keep it. But it's very expensive. Shouldn't I pay them something?"

"Oh, no. They'll just be glad the cat's found a good home."

With Mrs. Finney's thanks ringing in her

ears, Toni made her way back to the office.

"Well?" demanded Agatha.

"Simon found the cat and returned it," said Toni.

"Thank goodness for that."

Simon came in. "I'm glad you found that cat," said Agatha, "but there is other work here. Do not go off to Carsely again without telling me. I'll find you something else in the morning."

"Great!" said Simon.

"I'm leaving as well," said Toni. "Wait for me, Simon."

"We have to talk," said Toni. "What the hell were you about buying an expensive cat? I found the real one and took it back."

"Oh, God," said Simon. "Agatha'll be furious."

"I didn't tell her. The real cat had just been handed in at the centre. I told Mrs. Finney she could keep your cat as well. What on earth are you playing at?"

"Come for a drink," said Simon, "and I'll tell you."

Chapter Eight

Simon was longing for an excuse — any excuse — to talk about his idol. Toni listened with all the growing irritation of any woman listening to a young man lauding the beauties of another female.

When he had finally finished, Toni said, "Look, if this goes on you'll find yourself out of a job. Your heroine is one of the suspects — that is, if Agatha is right and the Frasers aren't murderers."

"Don't be silly. She's got cast-iron alibis. You're jealous!"

"Spare me," said Toni. "Your vanity is getting the better of you. Okay, if you want to shine in her eyes, why not try to be the detective who broke the case?"

Simon's odd, sometimes clownlike face lit up as he saw in his mind's eye himself standing beside Jessica, in front of the press, describing how he had found the real murderer.

"That's a great idea," he said. "I'll get on it right away."

"No, you won't," exclaimed Toni. "Do your work for Agatha or you won't have a job. If you must ferret around, do it in your own time."

Agatha Raisin drove home under a lowering sky. It looked as if the suffocating weather was about to break at last. She longed for a dramatic thunderstorm to match her racing mind. Somehow, she could feel in her very bones that the threat had not left Carsely although everyone she had talked to seemed to believe the danger was over. And the better-off villagers liked the idea of some criminal lowlifes from the estate being the villains.

Something told her Mrs. Glossop knew something. And what about the battered Mrs. Freemantle? Her husband was vicious enough.

She thought about the listening device in the office safe. It was tempting to think of using it. But listening illegally to people's private conversations was a dirty game.

As she drove down into Carsely, she could almost sense the overarching trees waiting for rain. There was a breathless stillness about the countryside. Agatha let herself into her cottage and patted her cats. She was just cooking liver for them when she realised she had never found out who inherited George's money. "What kind of detective am I?" she said to her indifferent cats.

When the liver was cooked, she set it aside to cool and phoned George's sister, Janet Ilston.

"What do you want?" demanded Janet.

"Who did George leave everything to?" asked Agatha.

"I don't know why you are still asking questions. I'm contesting his will. He left everything, including his cottage, to some female called Harriet Glossop."

"When did you find this out?" demanded Agatha.

"Yesterday."

"Why did you only find this out now?"

"An old army friend of his just back from Afghanistan turned up with the will. He had met George when he was last on leave and for some reason George gave him the will for safekeeping. It is one of those do-it-yourself wills you get from W. H. Smith."

"What is the name of this friend?"

"I don't see what it has to do with you."

"Because I think George may not have been murdered by the Frasers."

There was a long silence. "Hullo, hullo!"

said Agatha.

"I'm here. This is interesting. What if that Glossop woman murdered George for his money? Look, I'll rehire you."

"Okay. I'll send you the paperwork."

Agatha felt a surge of excitement after she had rung off. She decided to go and have a talk with Harriet Glossop.

The rain was coming down in sheets as she drove the short distance through the village to Harriet's cottage. The evening was very dark, the clouds above so low, they looked as if they were resting on the hills above Carsely.

As she got out of the car, she noticed a light was on in the living room. Agatha rang the doorbell and waited.

No reply.

She tilted her umbrella to get a view of the road. Harriet's Ford was parked next to the kerb. Agatha rang again.

The rain drummed on her umbrella and chuckled in the guttering of the cottage above her head. Agatha took out her mobile phone and scrolled through the logged numbers until she found Harriet's. She rang the number and then bent down and opened the letterbox. She could hear a phone ringing inside the house and then it switched over to voice mail.

Agatha experienced a frisson of unease. She carefully tried the door handle. The door was unlocked.

She swung the door open and called out, "Harriet! Are you there?"

Only the sound of the rain met her ears.

Then there was a sudden flash of lightning, so bright that for one awful moment Agatha thought the cottage had been struck. A light shone under the living-room door.

Harriet will walk in any moment and demand to know what the hell I am doing in her house, thought Agatha uneasily. Still . . . just a little look. She opened the living-room door.

It was a typical cottage living room with a chintz-covered sofa and two armchairs. A rather bad oil painting of a tabby cat hung over the fireplace. A display cabinet with pieces of china ornamented one corner. The round table by the window held the remains of a meal.

A glass of wine beside a dinner plate had been knocked over, spreading a red stain like blood over the white tablecloth.

A monumental crash of thunder made Agatha jump. Agatha took out her phone again and called Phil Marshall. "Phil," she said, "I'm at Harriet Glossop's cottage. I let myself in. She doesn't seem to be home but I've got a bad feeling. Before I search any further, could you come along here and join me?"

Phil said he would be along in a few minutes. Agatha sat down on the sofa and hugged her knees as the thunder rolled and crashed around the cottage.

It seemed to take an age until Phil arrived, although it was only five minutes.

"Are you sure she's not going to come back and find us trespassing?" asked Phil anxiously.

"We can always say we were worried about her," said Agatha. "Let's look around. I'll take the upstairs if you search the rest of the downstairs."

With a fast-beating heart, Agatha mounted the carpeted stairs. The first door she opened revealed what looked like the spare bedroom. She tried the next door and drew in a short sharp shocked breath before calling, "Phil!"

Phil Marshall came up the stairs with an agility that belied his years.

Harriet Glossop lay on her bed. A lamp burned on a bedside table. Her face was white and glistening with a deathly pallor in the light.

"I'd better check for a pulse," said Phil

nervously. He approached the bed and put a finger on Harriet's neck.

Harriet's eyes flew open and she let out a scream of pure terror.

"It's me, Agatha." Agatha moved forward into the light. "We rang the doorbell and phoned. We thought something awful had happened to you."

Harriet struggled up against the pillows and glared at them. "You're trespassing. I'll call the police."

"Don't do that," pleaded Agatha. "You must see how it looks. I learned that George had left everything in his will to you and . . . and . . . your face looks so white."

"It's anti-wrinkle cream," said Harriet, taking a tissue from a box on the bedside table and wiping her face. "And I take sleeping pills. I haven't been able to sleep properly since poor George's death."

Above their heads, the retreating storm was grumbling off into the distance.

"I'm going back to sleep," said Harriet. "Just get out of here."

"Can I make you a cup of tea?" said Agatha. "I'm sorry we gave you such a shock."

"Go away!" screamed Harriet.

Agatha and Phil retreated to Agatha's cottage. "Now I've done it," said Agatha gloomily. "I don't think she's going to want to speak to me ever again."

"Are you really sure the Frasers aren't the murderers?" asked Phil. "There's really no proof it was anyone else."

"I just have this feeling," said Agatha stubbornly. "I think this murderer is someone too clever and vicious to have been one of the Frasers. Why would someone want to murder Fiona, for example? I can imagine one of George's ex-lovers doing it in a jealous rage. But why the Frasers? This is only a village. Not a city. Who can creep about here, murdering Fiona in broad daylight in my garden . . ."

"You forget," interrupted Phil. "We believed, remember, that the murderer may have thought Fiona was you. And if the Frasers are not the murderers then there may be someone out there who still wants to kill you."

"Not as long as the Frasers are suspects. Whoever it is won't want the case opened again."

"Unless that someone is mad," said Phil.

"Let me think," said Agatha. "At first it seems impossible that someone could have dug up that rockery and put the snake books in that box without the neighbours, who initially reported the suspicious activities that led to the cannabis farm being discovered, noticing anything. On the other hand, what if the books were planted there *before* the murders as a safeguard. If the murderer felt the police were closing in, then an anonymous tip-off would have let them find that box. Which one of our few suspects could have known the Frasers?"

"Someone who smokes pot?" suggested Phil.

"If only I could interview the Frasers," wailed Agatha.

"They'll have a lawyer," said Phil. "Get his name and get him to ask them."

"Good idea. I'll do that tomorrow. Meantime, I'll see if Patrick can call on Harriet. He might have better luck."

"Tomorrow's Saturday," said Phil. "You'll probably need to wait till Monday to interview the lawyer."

"His name's probably on the Internet," said Agatha. "He's maybe quoted as making some sort of a statement."

Followed by Phil, she went through to her computer and switched it on. She scrolled through reports of the arrest of the Frasers. "Ah, here we are. Lawyer for the defence, Terence Ogilvie, said to the press, 'I cannot discuss the case at the moment.' I'll see if I can get his home number. Here is his office,

10 Market Street, Mircester. So with any luck he lives in Mircester. Pass me the Gloucestershire phone book."

She riffled quickly through the pages. "There's a T. Ogilvie at Fir Cottage, Harvey Road, Mircester. Good. I'll call on him tomorrow. Look at it this way. If planting those books was done before the murder, it could have been done when the husband was on the run and the wife was on remand."

"That can't be it," said Phil. "Mrs. Fraser dug the rockery after she was free."

"Rats! So she did. But wait a bit! That was still before the murders."

"It's all very far-fetched," said Phil.

"Have you ever known my intuition to be wrong before?" demanded Agatha.

"Yes."

Agatha's mind flew to all the mistakes she had made with men, and said hurriedly, "It won't do any harm just to see this lawyer. Phil, if you don't mind working at the weekend — you know I always pay overtime — could you ask the Frasers' neighbours if they saw anyone?"

"All right. Must get my beauty sleep."

Phil was in his late seventies but his thick white hair looked healthy and he had few lines on his face. Hope for me yet, thought Agatha. Mind you, Phil doesn't smoke.

Simon awoke on Saturday morning with a feeling of anticipation. Jessica would be in Carsely and he must think up a way of approaching her. But when he looked out of his window, he saw that it was a damp, drizzly day. He had hoped to be, say, strolling past her cottage and seeing her working in her front garden.

But Carsely drew him like a magnet. He set off in his car rather than on his motorbike, for the radio weather report in the morning had said that a lot of the roads were flooded.

He did not know that Toni was following him. Toni was worried about Simon. His obsession with Jessica had led him to being attacked outside the soap star's cottage.

Simon parked some distance away from Jessica's cottage. He began to wish he had put on some sort of disguise. What if Agatha should come across him?

He decided to stroll past Jessica's cottage. If her car was there then perhaps he could pluck up courage to ring the doorbell. Unlike Agatha, he believed the murders were solved so he couldn't even use the excuse of detecting.

Simon got out and began to walk. Toni, with a hood pulled down over her head and her face shielded by a large umbrella, set out in pursuit, but at some distance behind.

With a fast-beating heart, Simon saw that Jessica's car was there. He slowed his pace. Then an idea came to him. If he interviewed one of the women who had been involved with George, he might pick up a bit of gossip which would give him an excuse to call on Jessica.

He took out his BlackBerry and flicked through to notes on the case. Phil had also covertly snapped photos of suspects. Joyce Hemingway was described as acidulous and impossible to talk to. Harriet Glossop seemed approachable and her cottage was nearby.

Why is he going there? wondered Toni, watching him turn in at Harriet's gate. Like Simon had done, she flicked through her BlackBerry until she found the address. Harriet Glossop! He must have taken Agatha's theory seriously that the Frasers had not committed the murders.

Harriet's door was standing slightly open. Simon rang the bell. Water dripped mournfully from the thatch above his head and a hollyhock, crushed by last night's downpour, lay at his feet.

Determined to get some nugget of gossip to take to Jessica, he eased himself in the door. "Anybody home?" he called.

He thought he heard a movement from the kitchen at the back and moved slowly forward.

He stopped just before the kitchen and let out a gasp of horror. A woman lay prone on the floor, half in and half out of the kitchen, with blood pouring from a wound on the back of her head.

Simon was crouched down beside her, feeling for a pulse, when he was struck a massive blow.

Toni stood outside, wondering what to do. Then she decided to go and join him. If Simon had simply decided to go detecting, then she could as well.

Like Simon, she rang the bell. No reply. Surely they weren't out in the back garden on such a miserable day. She cautiously walked in, calling, "Simon!" as she went.

She thought she heard a faint groan coming from the back of the cottage and hurried forward.

Simon was lying prone over the body of a woman. Toni knelt down beside him. He made a choked sound. His pulse was weak and fluttering.

Toni called desperately for help. Then she phoned Agatha, stammering out the bad news. Agatha had been on her way to interview the lawyer when Toni rang.

Toni was frightened to move Simon in case she did more damage but did not want to leave him lying like that over the body of the woman. She gently eased him off and then ran upstairs to the bedroom and came back down with blankets to wrap around him. She soaked a clean dishtowel in the kitchen sink and held it to the bleeding wound on his head.

She heard Agatha arrive, and called, "Don't come any nearer. It's a crime scene and Simon has been badly hurt."

Agatha retreated to the road and paced up and down. She wished she had not told her staff that she did not believe the Frasers to be murderers. Simon must have decided to see what he could find out.

Police and ambulance arrived at the same time. After what was only about ten minutes but what seemed to Agatha like an age, Simon was carried out, a mask over his face.

"Will he live?" she asked one of the ambulance men.

"We need to get him to emergency right away. Stand clear," said the ambulance man impatiently.

Wilkes, Bill Wong and Alice Peterson were the next to arrive, followed by the Scenes of Crimes Operatives.

A white-faced Toni was called out to let SOCO do their job. She ran straight to Agatha, crying, "Simon looked near to death and Harriet Glossop has been murdered!"

"Now, then," said Wilkes, "what were you doing?"

"We didn't think the Frasers had done the murders," said Toni. "I knew Simon was going to do some detecting so I decided to follow him. He went into Harriet's and didn't come out so I followed him in and found him."

Overwrought, she burst into tears. "She's in shock," snarled Agatha. "Give her time to recover."

"We'll take her back to headquarters," said Wilkes.

"And I am coming, too, whether you like it or not," said Agatha.

While Toni was waiting to be interviewed, she whispered to Agatha, "I had to follow Simon because . . ."

"Miss Gilmour," a constable interrupted. "Come with me."

Why did she have to follow Simon? wondered Agatha. I hope there's no romantic interest there. He's just not suitable. He's too young and flighty.

"Agatha!"

Agatha looked up and saw the tall and handsome figure of her ex-husband James Lacey. He sat down beside her. "I just got back from my travels and heard the news. It's all over the village. I thought I might find you here."

Agatha clutched his hand. "Oh, James. It's such a mess. I was so sure the Frasers hadn't done those awful murders. I told my staff. Simon obviously wanted to do some detecting. When Harriet Glossop was murdered, the murderer must still have been in the house and attacked Simon. I don't know what Toni was doing following him. She found him and the dead body and now they're interviewing her."

"Toni should be in hospital being treated for shock," said James.

"I know. I'll take her straight there when they've finished with her."

But when Toni was finally escorted out by Bill Wong, Bill said, "Agatha, Inspector Wilkes would like a word with you."

"But Toni must go to hospital for a check. She's badly shocked. I must see that Simon is going to be all right."

"I'll take Toni," said James. "Meet us at the hospital."

Wilkes went through the usual recording preamble, and then said, "Why did you think the Frasers could not have committed the murders?" He looked at her crossly. This wretched woman had a way of bumbling around his cases and knocking them apart.

"Because the whole thing is too vicious and elaborate for one of them to have done it. It's just a hunch. George Marston left everything to Harriet Glossop. I think someone killed her in a jealous rage."

"And what does that intuition of yours tell you about the identity of the murderer?"

"I don't know. Is Sarah Freemantle's husband out on bail?"

"She won't press charges but has taken out an injunction against him."

"What about Joyce Hemingway?"

"Why her?"

"She's a nasty powerful sort of woman and she was having an affair with George. She was overheard threatening him. And what about Jessica Fordyce?"

"As there is no evidence at all that our beautiful soap star was romantically involved with Marston and has cast-iron alibis, perhaps your jealousy is taking over. It seems to be common knowledge in the village that you were obsessed with Marston. So where were you this morning?"

"At home."

"Witness?"

"My cats. Oh, I made several phone calls. You can check and I was at home when Toni called me."

"I want you to leave the police to do their job, Mrs. Raisin."

"You must admit this killing blows the case against the Frasers out of the water."

"That will be all, Mrs. Raisin."

"But . . ."

Wilkes turned to Bill Wong. "Get her out of here."

As they walked along the corridor outside the interview room, Bill said, "Look, Agatha, drop it. It's dangerous. I agree with you about the Frasers, but don't tell Wilkes. Some psycho is on the loose and if you're not careful, you'll be next."

Simon's parents were in the waiting room at the hospital. Mr. Black glared at Agatha. "If my son survives," he said, "I'll make sure he never works for you again."

"How is he?" asked James.

"They're operating on him. He has bleeding from the brain. Now, don't talk to me again. In fact, as you are not related to Simon, just get out of here."

"We are waiting for Miss Toni Gilmour, who found him and no doubt saved his life," said James. "She is with the hospital psychiatrist at the moment so we have every right to be here."

Never before had Agatha been so glad of James's support. She and James sat in a corner of the waiting room away from the Blacks.

Toni eventually appeared, still looking white and shaken. "He says I'll be all right but says I should come back for another consultation."

"Come home with me," urged Agatha.

"No, I would like to be on my own. If you could drive me back to Carsely, I left my car there."

"I don't think you're fit to drive it back to Mircester," said James.

"Let me alone," said Toni sharply. "I can look after myself."

In the days and weeks that followed, Agatha was too upset and weary to visit the lawyer. As sometimes a detective would say in one of her favourite documentaries, "And then the case went cold."

This case, thought Agatha, was not only

cold, it was in the deep freeze.

Tim Fraser, his wife and his son had been charged with concealing illegal earnings and had been released on bail.

The Cotswolds began to fill with tourists. The press had haunted Carsely for a week, questioning villagers. Half had hopes of being on television, the other half blamed Agatha Raisin, who, they felt, had brought all this murder and mayhem to the village.

Jessica Fordyce gave a television interview, saying that nothing would drive her from her beautiful cottage.

Simon made a rapid recovery and, as soon as he was released from hospital, was taken on holiday by his parents.

The Timmons agency had packed up and left and Agatha took on several of their cases. James was off on his travels again and Charles showed no signs of visiting her.

As July moved into August, Roy Silver phoned and said he hoped to visit her at the week-end. Agatha often found the young man irritating but, for once eagerly looked forward to his company. Mrs. Bloxby was off on a rare holiday to Majorca and Agatha felt she had no one to talk to. Toni rebuffed all her concern and looked closed down.

Because of the workload, Agatha had been working over the week-ends, but decided to take the next one off when Roy would arrive.

The weather was summery once more, with great fleecy clouds crossing a blue sky and shadows racing up and down the Cotswold hills.

Roy had gone in for a mahogany tan. He was wearing an open-necked white shirt and white trousers. As he went to meet Agatha in the station car park, he hoped someone would take him for a film star, but a grouchy old man, walking past him with his wife, mumbled, "Bloody Asians. They're everywhere."

"Did you hear what he said?" complained Roy.

"Yes, but you are very dark," said Agatha. "Don't you worry about skin cancer?"

"That's a myth."

"And smoking doesn't give you lung cancer. Do you want to eat at home, or have lunch somewhere?"

"Dine out, please," said Roy. "It's too hot for one of your microwave curries."

They had lunch in the garden of the White Hart Royal, an old Royalist pub in Moreton-in-Marsh where once King Charles I had fled without paying his bill.

"Tell me all about it," said Roy when they had reached the coffee stage.

"I don't know that I want to," said Agatha. "I've an awful feeling this is going to go down as one of my failures."

"Out with it, babes," said Roy. "Not like you to give up."

Agatha sighed but then began to talk. When she had finished, Roy said, "What I can't understand is that, according to Jessica, Joyce Hemingway was heard screaming at George that she would kill him. And according to Simon, Jessica said that Joyce once worked at London Zoo. Yet, you don't seem to have interviewed her yourself."

"I can't get near her. She just insults me."

"Yes, but the police must have done. They must have been round the village interviewing everyone, and that would include this Mrs. Arnold, who reported she had heard Joyce threatening George and then told Jessica. Maybe Bill Wong would tell us."

"I'm sick of the whole thing," said Agatha pettishly. "I've just begun to get a good night's sleep without imagining snakes slithering everywhere."

"Not like you to get scared off," said Roy.

"Okay," said Agatha wearily. "He might be at home. I'd better ring first."

Bill said he would meet them at a café in the square at Mircester. When he arrived to join them, he looked tired. "Wilkes hasn't given up, Agatha," he said. "He's got some of us going over and over all the interviews, trying to find a lead. He still hopes it'll turn out to be the Frasers."

"I've been going over my own notes," said Agatha. She moved her chair out of the sun. "Don't want to get a tan. So unfashionable."

"You're only saying that because to a woman of your years, it's ageing. Flattering in a young man like me," said Roy.

"Bitch!"

"Children, children," admonished Bill. "What did you want to see me about?"

"It's about Joyce Hemingway," said Agatha. "Mrs. Arnold reported that she had been heard screaming at George that she would kill him."

"I remember. I've just been reading that again on the notes," said Bill. "She denies the whole thing and Mrs. Arnold backed down and said she must have been mistaken. She looked frightened. We pressed her but she refused to budge. Joyce Hemingway was pretty rude. Asked if she knew anything about snake handling, she said that she had worked as a secretary at London Zoo and had had nothing to do with any reptiles or animals. Checked back and found someone who knew her. That seems to have been the case. She was fired for insolence."

"What about the snake books found under the rockery?" asked Agatha. "Any fingerprints?"

"None."

"Well, that should have looked suspicious from the start. Were the Frasers' fingerprints found on that box?"

"Yes."

"There you are. Didn't that make the police suspicious? Why wipe the books clean and leave their prints on the box?"

"Look, Agatha, I've got to get back to work. If there is a murderer out there, you could be at risk. Just drop it."

"Nothing's happened for ages," said Agatha mulishly. "Someone's sitting smugly somewhere thinking they've got away with it."

"Then let them think it and leave the whole thing to the police. How's Simon?"

"Back at work. His father said he would cut off his allowance if he continued to work as a detective, but Simon insisted on going on with it. He seems obsessed with Jessica Fordyce. I can't understand it."

"You should understand obsession more than anyone else, Agatha," said Roy.

"Shut up, or you'll have to walk back to Carsely."

Toni was wishing she had not volunteered to come on this outing. Simon had suggested they take a picnic up to the Malvern Hills. Toni had agreed to go with him because she was worried about him. He seemed to be almost feverishly excited and she wondered if he had fully recovered from his injury. The sun beat down on them.

"I've always sneered at global warming," said Simon, "but this is an exceptional summer."

"Don't worry. Now the scientists say we are heading for another mini ice age," said Toni. "Can we find a bit of shade and sit down?"

"Just a bit farther."

Toni was getting tired and cross despite the spectacular views. The Malvern Hills were open to the public and were crisscrossed with about one hundred miles of footpaths and bridleways. Toni was beginning to feel they had walked them all.

Simon stopped abruptly on the crest of a rise. "Would you look at that!" he said. "Someone's filming."

"Oh, surprise, surprise," said Toni cynically. "I do wonder if it's Jessica Fordyce."

But Simon was off and running, clutching a travel bag containing their picnic. He only asked me along as camouflage, thought Toni. She followed more slowly.

She saw Simon going into a large catering van and glanced at her watch. Lunchtime. The cast must be taking a break.

Jessica was sitting at a table with a young man who was glaring up at Simon. "Who's this?" asked Jessica as Toni walked in. "Your girlfriend?"

"Oh, no," said Simon. "Just a young coworker. I'm taking her out for a picnic as a break. May I talk to you?"

"Come outside and we'll find somewhere in the shade. You haven't introduced me."

Simon scowled. "This is Toni Gilmour."

"Hi, Toni. Why don't you get something to eat and join Rex Dangerfield here while I talk to Simon?"

"I'll get a drink," said Toni, glaring at Simon, "but we've got food with us and it would be a shame to waste it."

Jessica settled herself in a chair outside the catering van and Simon sat next to her. "What's this episode about?" asked Simon.

"Oh, I have one of my stormy breakups with Rex. Same old, same old."

"Do you ever think of quitting the show?"

"Often. But I've seen what happens to

other actors who quit long-running series. I'm too identified with the character of nurse Maggie. It would be hard to find anything else. Why are you really here?"

To worship you would have been the correct answer, but Simon said, "Just by chance."

"So the Frasers are in the clear?"

"Oh, them, yes."

"Odd, that."

"It looked like them until Harriet Glossop was attacked. Me as well."

"Poor you. I read about that." She smiled at him bewitchingly. "Are you all right now?"

"Oh, yes," breathed Simon.

To Simon's irritation, Toni and Rex came to join them. "Time to get our make-up repaired," said Rex.

"You can stay and watch if you like," said Jessica.

Toni began, "I think we should be getting along because . . ."

"We'd love to," said Simon.

Toni suddenly let out a scream. "Snake!" she cried, and pointed.

An adder was slithering through the tussocky grass.

Jessica seized a furled parasol which was beside her chair, put the point under the snake and neatly flipped it away.

"Come on, Rex," she said.

Toni sank down onto the chair Jessica had vacated, and whispered, "Did you see that?"

"So brave," said Simon. "I was terrified. Let's go and watch the filming."

"I'll follow you."

Toni waited until he had left and then took out her phone and called Agatha.

"I'm up in the Malvern Hills with Simon. He said we were to go on a picnic but it turns out he's stalking Jessica. But listen to this!" She told Agatha how deftly Jessica had coped with the snake.

When she had finished, Agatha said, "I'd been taking the police's word for it about her alibis. I'm going to check every one of them out."

As the hot day of filming dragged on and Toni nervously scanned the ground for adders, she began to wish she had not agreed to come in Simon's car.

At last Simon joined her. His eyes were glowing. "The crew are heading back to London," he said, "but get this! Jessica has invited me for dinner."

"And me?" asked Toni.

"Er, no," lied Simon, who had said that Toni had a date.

"Look, Simon, I told Agatha how nifty Jessica had been in getting rid of that adder."

"You what?"

"Well, don't you find it suspicious?"

"No, I do not," raged Simon. "I want Agatha to leave her alone."

"She's just going to go over Jessica's alibis again."

"I wish I'd never brought you," said Simon sulkily.

"The feeling's mutual. Now we've got the long walk back."

"The road's just over there. The sound man says he'll give us a lift back to my car."

Simon was silent on the road back to Mircester. All he wanted to do was to get rid of Toni and pick out something to wear.

Once in Mircester, Toni went to her own car and drove to Carsely.

"Any luck with those alibis?" asked Toni when Agatha answered the door.

"I've got Roy here on a visit. I decided we'll all get onto it on Monday. Where is Simon?"

"He's been invited to Jessica's for dinner. I'm worried about him."

"Come into the garden and have a drink and say hullo to Roy."

Roy seemed almost as infatuated with Jessica as Simon. "If you ask me," he whispered as Agatha went to get Toni a glass of mineral water, "Agatha's just jealous of Jessica. I mean Jessica's enough to make any woman jealous."

"Not me," said Toni.

CHAPTER NINE

Simon, dressed in his best suit, striped shirt and silk tie, nervously rang the doorbell of Jessica's cottage that evening.

At first he thought she was not at home, but then he heard scuffling sounds from behind the door and a male voice shouting, "Don't answer it and maybe he'll go away."

Must think it's a reporter, thought Simon, and rang the bell again.

There was a silence and then the door was suddenly opened. Jessica stood there. She was wearing denim shorts with a man's shirt tied round her waist and she was in her bare feet.

"Why, Simon!" she cried.

"You did invite me for dinner, didn't you?" asked Simon.

"Did I? It's been such a hectic day, I must have forgotten. Come in anyway and have a drink. 'Fraid I can't do dinner."

Simon felt snubbed. A little voice of common sense was telling him to leave, but she smiled so prettily that he said, "Well, all right."

She led the way into the kitchen. To his annoyance, Rex was there. "You're all dressed up," he said, surveying Simon. "If it wasn't a Saturday, I'd guess you'd been to see your bank manager."

"I did think I was invited to dinner," said Simon. Rex was naked to the waist, showing a trim, muscled body.

"I'm afraid we've eaten," said Rex, indicating an empty pizza box on the table.

"Run along, Rex," said Jessica. "I'll just have a drink with Simon and then we can get back to rehearsing our lines."

Rex slouched out of the kitchen. "What'll you have?" asked Jessica.

"I'll just have a black coffee," said Simon. "I'm driving."

She went to a gleaming espresso machine and began to prepare his coffee.

"So," said Jessica when she had set a cup of coffee on the kitchen table, "sit down and tell me what you've been detecting."

"Oh, just bread-and-butter stuff," said Simon. "Divorces, lost teenagers, things like that."

"No murders?"

"Nothing like that."

"What about George's murder?"

"Dead end, I'm afraid," said Simon, "but Agatha is very tenacious."

"But what on earth can she do that the police can't?"

"I really don't know. But somehow she digs away and bumbles around and always comes up with something."

"Isn't she afraid?"

"I think Agatha's curiosity is bigger than her fear. Let's talk about you. I thought your acting was superb this afternoon."

She shrugged. "It's a job. I'm lucky. Look, I'm sorry I forgot about dinner, but I'm worried about Rex."

"Why?" asked Simon jealously.

"We haven't got to the end of the next script. In it, he's killed off. He's going to be furious."

"What did he do before?"

"Not much. Shaving advertisement, that sort of thing. He's been throwing his weight around a bit much on set, so they decided to write him out."

"That's a bit hard. I mean, to let him find out like that. Couldn't they just give him a warning?"

"He's had several warnings. Now, you really must go."

Simon rose reluctantly to his feet. She

walked him to the door and kissed him on the cheek. "Maybe another time," she said.

As the door closed, he stood miserably on the step. Then he sensed he was being watched and turned round.

Joyce Hemingway stood there. He walked down the path to join her. "What are you staring at?" demanded Simon.

"You men are a joke, the way you sniff around her," said Joyce harshly.

"I don't suppose many men sniff around you," said Simon. "By the way, you were overheard threatening to kill George Marston."

"That's a lie!" she said passionately. "George loved me!"

"And half the village as well," commented Simon.

She slapped him full across the face so hard that he had to hang on to the garden gate for support. Then she set off down the road with long athletic strides.

Simon got into his car and drove to Agatha's cottage. Toni, Roy and Agatha had just finished dinner.

"I'm hungry," said Simon when he joined them in the kitchen.

"I thought you were having dinner with Jessica," said Toni.

"Cancelled. Said she had to rehearse with

the poisonous Rex. She says he'll find out at the end of the script that he's been killed off."

"And you all dressed up and nowhere to go."

Simon shrugged. "I had a confrontation with the terrible Joyce. She slapped my face."

"What did you say?" asked Agatha.

"I told her she'd been heard threatening to kill George. She said George loved her, and I said, 'Yes, and half the village as well.' "

"She's dangerous," said Toni.

"Keep away from her," urged Agatha.

"I'm bored," said Roy pettishly. He loved more than anything to see his photo in the newspapers and he had hoped the press would still be around the village. "I'm going for a walk."

"Suit yourself." Agatha turned to Simon. "There's some of a lamb casserole left that Mrs. Bloxby gave me. Like some?"

"That would be great."

As Roy walked through the village under a violet evening sky, he found his steps leading him to Jessica's cottage. He wondered whether he could persuade her to take him on as a publicist. Then he could return to

London on Monday to present that success to his boss at the public relations agency.

He put his hand on her garden gate and then stopped short. There came the sound of breaking glass and china and a man's voice shouting, "How dare you let them plan to kill me off!"

Roy took out his mobile phone and dialled Mircester police headquarters.

"Listen!" said Toni. "I think I hear police sirens."

They all went out to the front of Agatha's cottage. "There are blue lights up the hill. That's where Joyce lives. Come on!" said Agatha.

But they found three police cars outside Jessica's cottage, not Joyce's. A furious Jessica was standing on the doorstep while a shamefaced Roy was being lectured by Wilkes.

Agatha arrived in time to hear Wilkes say to Roy, "They were rehearsing a script. Didn't you think to check before you wasted police time?"

"But I heard all this commotion and the sound of things breaking," pleaded Roy.

"Miss Fordyce has clearly explained they were getting into their parts. I should book you for wasting police time."

"Come along, Roy," said Agatha. "I am sure he is very sorry and it won't happen again."

Back in her kitchen, Agatha said, "Don't you remember, Roy, before you went out, Simon explained that Rex was about to discover that he'd been killed off in the latest script?"

"I don't believe that was all there was to it. He was shouting, 'How dare you plan to let them kill me off.' Then I could hear what sounded like crockery and glass being smashed."

"They could have had a tape of sound effects," said Toni.

"Well, if that line's in the script, I'll eat my hat."

"The new series doesn't run until next October," said Simon. "You won't know until then."

"Did you never consider, Simon, that Rex and Jessica might be lovers?" asked Toni.

"He's gay," said Roy.

"You don't know that," said Simon.

"Trust me. I know."

Sulkily deciding that there was no hope of any publicity, Roy took himself off early the next day.

Agatha, finding herself on her own, decided to visit Mrs. Bloxby. This time she phoned first, but Mrs. Bloxby said she would rather call on Agatha as her husband was busy, it being Sunday, which Agatha translated as meaning that Alf Bloxby's temporary feelings of goodwill towards her had evaporated.

As she waited for her friend, Agatha wondered what Charles was doing. Perhaps he blamed her for the breakup with Petronella.

When Mrs. Bloxby arrived, Agatha served her with her favourite glass of dry sherry and helped herself to a gin and tonic.

"What was all the fuss about at Miss Fordyce's cottage?" asked Mrs. Bloxby.

Agatha told her about Rex losing his part.

"Oh, he's not losing it," said Mrs. Bloxby. "Haven't you read the Sunday papers?"

"I haven't been along to get them yet."

"Miss Fordyce has made a statement that if Rex leaves the show, then so does she."

Agatha's bearlike eyes gleamed with excitement. "I wonder if he's got some sort of hold over her."

"They are reported to be lovers."

"Roy says that Rex is gay."

"I suppose he could be," said Mrs. Bloxby. "It's a sad fact that in England good-looking young men with superb figures often are."

"And," pointed out Agatha, "who knows better than I how to spin a story for the newspapers. Maybe we're looking at this the wrong way round. Maybe Jessica is one of those women who falls in love with the unattainable."

And you know what it's like to keep falling in love with the unattainable, thought Mrs. Bloxby, but did not voice the thought aloud.

"Maybe," Agatha went on, "Jessica was eaten up with jealousy and used Rex as her creature to get rid of the rivals."

"I really don't think either of them has anything to do with it," said Mrs. Bloxby. "Miss Fordyce is so beautiful that surely she could have had an affair with Mr. Marston if she wanted to."

"Perhaps she wanted to and couldn't," said Agatha excitedly. "George had a penchant for the more mature woman." Except me, she thought. "I'd like to get a close look at both of them. I might call on them today."

"Oh, do be careful!"

As Agatha walked up to Jessica's cottage, she noticed the day was quite chilly and a thin veil of white cloud was covering the sky. The disadvantage of living in the country, she thought, was one was too aware of the changing seasons and it would soon be autumn again, reminding a middle-aged woman like herself of things ageing and dying.

The countryside was very quiet except for the faint sound of a tractor on the hills above the village.

Agatha squared her shoulders, walked up the path and rang the doorbell. Jessica opened the door, looked her up and down, and said curtly, "I'm busy. Go away."

"Just a few words," pleaded Agatha. "I won't take up much of your time."

Jessica shut the door in her face.

Agatha walked slowly away. She saw the unlovely figure of Mrs. Arnold approaching. Mrs. Arnold blocked her path. "That poor girl," she said. "The press have been bothering her all morning and now you."

"And where are the press now?"

"In the pub, getting drunk."

"Good idea," said Agatha. "I'll join them."

Reporters and cameramen were clustered around tables outside the Red Lion, smoking and drinking.

"Here's Aggie!" shouted a reporter from *The Morning Record*. "Any news?"

Agatha pulled a chair up next to him.

"Not a thing. Who is this Rex Dangerfield that Jessica should risk her career standing up for him?"

"Nasty git," said another reporter. "Usually preens himself the minute he sees a camera but not today."

"Do me a favour," said Agatha. "Does Rex have an address in London or does he live in Jessica's flat?"

"I'm Reg Hendry," said the *Morning Record* reporter. "Come inside to the bar. I'll buy you a drink. I help you and you help me."

"Okay." Agatha followed him into the darkness of the old pub. Reg bought her a gin and tonic and a pint for himself. He was a tired-looking man in his thirties with thinning brown hair and blurred features as if many pints of beer had softened the lines. He was wearing a blue open-necked shirt and faded jeans. Agatha remembered when reporters always used to wear suits.

They took their drinks to a table in a corner by the window. "I'll give you his London address and what I have on him," said Reg, "on condition you tell me if you find out anything that would make a good story."

"It's a deal," said Agatha.

He took a gulp of beer, and then said, "He

was born Rex Pratt. Parents lived in Lewisham. Poor and dishonest. Mother had several charges for shoplifting and father for burglary. He worked on building sites and then got a job, no one knows how, as a tour operator taking people round India. Then he signed up with an advertising agency and got some ads for shaving cream and toothpaste. Changed his name to Rex Dangerfield. Producer of the hospital soap took him on at first in a bit part as a junior doctor. Almost immediately he got a shed-load of fan mail so producer, Malcolm Fryer, upped him to star opposite Jessica. Publicity put out rumours that he and Jessica were an item."

"Do you think he's gay?" asked Agatha.

"Could be. But no one's heard anything about that."

"Address?"

Reg took out his iPhone and flicked through it. "Here we are. Number five, Chepstow Lane, Notting Hill."

Agatha took a note of it.

"Do your best," said Reg. "I'll be going back without a story."

"Well," said Agatha, "you could slant it this way. Village still in fear. Murders unsolved. Even Jessica Fordyce frightened to open her door. You never know who might be calling on you in this once rural idyll and blah, blah, blah. Terrified villagers frightened of snakes."

"Good idea. I'll join the others, wait till they pack up and get my photographer to take some pictures. Want to give me a quote?"

"Not me," said Agatha. "The police have told me to keep out of it."

Agatha returned to her cottage, depressed because the other members of the press had shown no interest in her. She was yesterday's news.

She saw Charles's car outside her cottage. He had a set of keys and had let himself in. He was sitting in the garden with both cats on his lap.

"Nice to see you," said Agatha. "Haven't seen you for a bit."

"Doing this and that. Bring me up to speed on the unsolved murders."

He listened carefully and when Agatha had finished, he said, "What do you plan to do?"

"I think I'll go up to London tomorrow and watch his flat. I want to see what he does, where he goes and who his friends are."

"I'm bored. I'll come with you."

"Are you finished with Petronella?"

"Of course." Charles suddenly grinned. "Private detectives. They're all over the place."

"We'd better check tomorrow morning and make sure Jessica's car's gone. No point in going to London if the pair of them are still down here. And I'll see if Reg knows which tour company he worked for. I'd like to know if he got sacked for something."

Agatha went into her office the following morning to allocate work. "Where are you off to?" asked Simon.

"Just chasing a lead," said Agatha. "I'll let you know if anything comes of it."

Simon had plans of his own. He had taken the phone number of the make-up girl, Hattie Chivers, while he had been watching the filming in the Malverns. He had phoned her up and had arranged to meet her for dinner in London that evening. He wanted to find out as much as he could about the relationship between Jessica and Rex.

Toni watched him anxiously. She planned to keep an eye on him. She felt sure Simon was going to do something very silly — or dangerous.

Rex lived in a mews house in Chepstow

Lane. Charles was driving and managed to squeeze his old BMW into a parking space opposite Rex's house.

Through a slit in the downstairs curtains, they could see a light burning. But it was the sort of thing people did for security when they went out. If Rex had already gone out on the town for the evening, thought Agatha, it was going to be a long wait.

But after ten minutes, a taxi drove up and Rex got out. He went into his house but the taxi stayed outside with the meter running. "Get ready to follow the taxi," said Agatha.

After a short time, Rex came out and the taxi drove off. Charles waited until it reached the end of the lane and then began to follow.

After some time, when the taxi began to cross Westminster Bridge, Agatha said impatiently, "Where on earth is he going?"

"Need to keep after him till we find out," said Charles placidly.

The taxi went on into Lambeth, turned down a side street and stopped in front of a club called Pink Peter. "I think that answers the question of whether he's gay or not," said Charles. "I'd better park and go in after him. I hope he doesn't know what I look like. You'll have to wait for me."

"Will you be safe?" asked Agatha anxiously.

"I'll be safer in a gay club than I'd be in some pubs I know," said Charles. "Wish me luck."

As he cautiously approached, Charles saw that young men going in were holding up membership disks. He hung back until a noisy crowd arrived and joined them. He eased into the centre of the group, and was swept in past the doorman.

Rex was sitting at the bar with a young man. Charles took a seat at the far end of the bar. A few couples were dancing on a small dance floor. The music was Cole Porter. It all seemed very discreet and retro. Blown-up photos of Marlene Dietrich and Judy Garland in *The Wizard of Oz* decorated the walls.

"Well, if it isn't Charles Fraith," said a voice in his ear.

Charles stared up at the beefy features of someone he knew. "Why, Buffy!" he exclaimed. "What are you doing here?"

"Same as you," said Bernard Buff-Jerryn.

"Didn't know you were a friend of Dorothy's," said Charles. "Aren't you married?"

"What's that got to do with it?" demanded Buffy.

"Just wondered." Rex and the young man got to their feet, went to a staircase in the corner of the room and began to mount the stairs. "What's up there?" asked Charles.

"Rooms for a bit of you-know-what. Interested?"

"Not me. Wasn't that Rex Dangerfield who just went upstairs?"

"Yes. We get a lot of celebs in here. This your first time?" Buff put a heavy hand on Charles's knee.

Charles gently removed it. "I'm detecting, Buffy."

"You can't do that! The thing about this club is that it's the most discreet in London. I've got my reputation to consider. I'm a Liberal MP, or have you forgotten?"

"I won't say a word, Buffy. Does Rex come here a lot?"

"I'm off. If you aren't out of here in the next few minutes, I'm getting you thrown out," said Buffy.

Charles slid off the bar stool and made his way to the door and out into the street.

"I daren't wait any longer," said Charles when he joined Agatha. "Rex is definitely gay. I met an old school friend. Last person you would suspect. Roly-poly politician, wife and two kids. What do we do now?"

"Let's go somewhere for dinner," said Agatha. "I've a feeling I've been looking at this case the wrong way around."

Simon and Hattie Chivers were having dinner in Rules in Covent Garden. Looking down the prices on the menu, Simon could only be glad that his parents had relented and had reinstated his allowance.

Hattie was thin to the point of emaciation. Her arms were like sticks. Her brown hair was lank. She asked him to order. Simon ordered the most inexpensive items on the menu, fearing that anything more expensive would turn out to be a waste of food. This turned out to be the case, as Hattie merely picked at her fish.

"Now," said Simon eagerly, after he had heard all Hattie's complaints about working for the soap, "How do you get on with Jessica?"

"No one gets on with Jessica," said Hattie. "She's a right cow."

"She struck me as charming."

"Well, she would. She does this warmth and friendliness but she's always trying to put the knife into someone. You have to be sure to pay homage to her or she'll get you fired. The producer, Malcolm, is so terrified of losing her that he'll do anything she wants. There was this old actor Carl Friend. Hadn't had a part in forever and couldn't believe his luck when he landed the role of lovable old patient. One day, Jessica was late on the set, and Carl joked, 'Come on, Jessie, move yer bloody arse.' He was only quoting from *My Fair Lady*. The next thing we know, he's been written out."

"But that could have been the producer's decision."

"No. I overheard Jessica whispering to him, 'That'll teach you to watch what you say in the future.' "

"I can hardly believe it," said Simon.

"Men can't, until they get wise to her."

"What's her relationship with Rex Dangerfield?"

Hattie hid a piece of fish under her vegetables. "The terrible twosome. They make a vicious combination. Always trying to throw the other actors off. Malcolm, the producer, thought if he could get rid of Rex, the atmosphere might get better, but Jessica ups and says she'll leave the series if he goes."

"Is he gay?"

"Is the Pope Catholic?"

"So why are they so close?"

"I think our Jessica's a psycho," said Hattie. "Got to go and powder my nose."

She's jealous, that's all, thought Simon. But he flicked through the notes on his phone, coming across the bit where George had asked Agatha if she knew anything about psychos.

Hattie eventually came back. Her face was white and covered with a thin film of sweat. Probably been to throw up, thought Simon cynically.

"Aren't you jealous of her?" asked Simon.

"I thought you invited me out because you liked me," complained Hattie, "but you're just another poor sod who thinks Jessica's a goddess. Well, thanks but no thanks for dinner." She got up and marched out of the restaurant.

"It's like this," said Agatha as she and Charles dined at a Turkish restaurant in Borough High Street. "So Rex is gay. Now what if he was the one that had been in love with George? Maybe George swung both ways."

"I can't see it. He had a penchant for motherly women."

"Oh, yeah? What about Joyce Hemingway?"

"We've only got her word for it that she and George were an item," said Charles.

Agatha's phone rang. "Hello, Simon,"

Charles heard her say. Then Agatha listened intently. Then she said, "Come and join us for coffee." She gave him directions.

When she had rung off, she said, "Simon's just had dinner with the make-up girl from the soap. He says he might have something interesting."

When Simon joined them, Agatha asked eagerly what he had found out. Simon finished by saying, "Of course, she's an anorexic wimp and probably as jealous as hell."

Agatha's eyes gleamed with excitement. "Suppose she's telling the truth and her producer would do anything to keep Jessica sweet. He may even have lied to the police about where she was at significant times and given her those alibis."

"Why don't we just tell Bill Wong what we've got," said Simon uneasily, "and let the police get on with it?" He had not got over the shock of being bitten by an adder.

"What would they do?" demanded Agatha. "Same as before. The producer, Malcolm Fryer, will stick to his guns and there's nothing they can do about it. Do you know if they are on location tomorrow, Simon?"

"As a matter of fact, they're going back to the Malvern Hills."

"I'll see what I can do," said Agatha, her eyes gleaming with excitement. "I don't need to be landed with a long walk like you and Toni had. I'll go by the route near the road that they take."

"I'll come with you," said Simon eagerly.

"No," said Agatha. "You're too smitten with Jessica to see straight. Charles and I will go."

"Can't," said Charles. "Hosting the village cricket match."

When Charles dropped her off at her cottage, Agatha had a sudden weak longing to beg him to stay. In the excitement of the new discovery, she had forgotten her night-time fear of adders. It was almost as if Charles had sensed what she wanted to say because his face wore a closed-down, shuttered look. He gave her a brief goodbye and drove off.

Agatha let herself into her cottage, petted her cats and trailed into the kitchen. She phoned Toni and told her all about the latest developments and asked the girl to accompany her on the following day. Toni arranged to meet Agatha in the office at nine in the morning. "What time do they start filming?" she asked.

"I forgot to ask Simon and I don't want

to phone him. He's so besotted he might turn up."

"These location things usually take all day," said Toni. "We'll set off at nine."

That night there was a tremendous thunderstorm. Agatha tossed and turned, imagining snakes slithering down from the thatch and under the doors. Her cats joined her on her bed. At last the storm rolled away and she fell into an uneasy sleep.

When she joined Toni in the office, she again felt a pang of envy as she surveyed the girl's good looks and glowing healthy face. She looked at her own face in a mirror on the wall. She had dark shadows under her eyes and the lines on either side of her mouth seemed more pronounced. Not so long ago, thought Agatha, women of my age just let themselves go. They let the lines come and the hair go grey and the figure to droop and thicken. I need a complete body transplant.

"How are you going to go about this?" asked Toni as they drove off in Agatha's car.

"I'll work my way round to it," said Agatha uneasily, because she had not really worked out a plan of campaign. "Maybe I'll let you try to chat him up."

"You should have warned me," said Toni.

"I'm not wearing chat-up clothes."

She was dressed in shorts and a striped T-shirt, her long legs ending in sandals.

"At your age and with your looks," sighed Agatha, "it doesn't matter what you wear."

The day looked as if it had been washed clean by the storm. Water glittered on the leaves on the trees as the sun shone down from a clear sky. Agatha switched on the radio and then almost immediately switched it off again. "If there's one thing I can't stand," she said, "it's cheeky chappie DJs who sing along with the records or talk through them. That man is a garrulous prick."

"Want me to try Classic FM?" asked Toni.

"No, don't bother. Full of ads."

"What about Radio 3?"

"You can forget that one as well. Some pontificating moron will be saying something like, 'We will now play a piece of music not often heard by Austrian composer, Freidrich Bummergritch,' or something like that and I feel like screaming that the reason it's not often heard is because nobody wants to hear the damn thing."

Agatha relapsed into silence and drove steadily on. She found herself thinking about that listening device in the office safe. So easy just to take the thing out and bring it along. No wondering about which questions to ask.

At that very moment, Simon was thinking about the listening device as well. He wanted to see Jessica. Did she ever talk about him? His duties for the day lay in finding one cat and one dog. He began to speculate that Agatha would not mind if he said he could not find them and would try again the next day. To make sure, all the same, he checked with the animal shelter. He managed to find the dog and returned it to its grateful owners. No sign of the cat. He phoned the cat's owner to see if she had any news and heard to his delight that the cat had returned home.

Now, the listening device drew him like a magnet. He staked out the office until he saw Mrs. Freedman leaving for lunch and then went cautiously upstairs. The office door was locked, which meant that Patrick and Phil were out as well. He unlocked the door and went in. He went quickly to the safe and put in the combination — a combination that Agatha had left on a piece of paper in the top drawer of her desk.

He was just lifting out the machine when he heard footsteps coming up the stairs. He grabbed the listening device, quickly re-locked the safe and scurried into the toilet in the corner of the office.

He heard someone come in and the rustle of paper. Then a knock at the toilet door. Mrs. Freedman's voice. "Who's in there?"

"It's me, Simon."

"Can you hurry up?"

"I've got constipation."

"I can't wait much longer."

"Coming!"

Simon put the machine under his jacket and zipped it up. He emerged, clutching his stomach.

"Are you all right?" asked Mrs. Freedman. "I decided to buy a sandwich and have my lunch in the office."

"Yes, a bit of tummy trouble."

When she went into the toilet, Simon scurried down the stairs and headed for his motorbike. If anyone opened the safe and found it gone, he would say he took it home to be on the safe side, or that he could sell it on eBay, or something like that. The day was fine and at the end of the road to the Malvern Hills was his goddess. He stowed the machine in his bike and roared off.

When Agatha and Toni arrived, there were a few sightseers, standing at the perimeter, taking photographs.

They edged forward to get nearer to the filming. A security guard barred their way. "You can't come any closer," he ordered.

"Oh, yes we can," said Agatha. "We're guests of Malcolm Fryer."

"All right then, but be quiet."

Toni and Agatha edged as close as they could. "We'll just do that scene again," Malcolm was saying. "Jessica has been bitten by an adder. Rex, you go frantic because you can't get your mobile to work. So you've got to suck out the poison."

"Right. Cool," said Rex. "Why can't we use a real adder? I've got one here."

"For God's sake, get rid of it. Health and Safety would go bananas. We're going to cut to a library shot of an adder. What if she really got bitten?"

"I know how to handle snakes," said Rex sulkily.

"Forget it. Silence everybody. Camera. Action."

Just at that moment, Rex looked across and saw Agatha and Toni. "What's she doing here?" he shouted.

The producer swung round. "It's that amateur nosey tec from the village," said Rex. "I can't act with her around."

Malcolm strode up to them. "I must ask you to leave. What are you doing here?"

"I'm wondering why you lied to the police about Jessica's alibis," said Agatha.

Toni suppressed a groan. And to think Agatha often prided herself on what she saw as her tact and diplomacy.

"Don't be ridiculous!" raged Malcolm. "Just get the hell out of here!"

Jessica came up to them. "What's up?"

"This wretched woman is claiming that I lied to give you alibis."

Jessica gave a silvery laugh. "Oh, that's our Agatha for you. Agatha, why don't you wait in my trailer? We'll sort all this out later." She signalled to the security guard. "Show these ladies to my trailer."

"But . . ." began Malcolm.

"Don't worry about it," said Jessica. "All will be explained."

Agatha and Toni sat in Jessica's trailer and waited . . . and waited. "I'm hungry," complained Toni.

As if on cue, the door of the trailer opened and a girl entered carrying a tray. "Miss Fordyce said you might like to eat something. She says she'll only be about another hour."

"Where did you get this food from?" asked Agatha suspiciously.

"I collected it from catering," said the girl,

looking surprised.

When the girl had left, Agatha eyed the tray of chicken sandwiches and coffee. "Come on," said Toni. "She's not going to poison us with all these people around. And at least we can now tell the police that Rex knows how to handle adders."

They ate and drank, listening to the noise of the cast and extras outside. Agatha's vision began to blur and her head swam. "Toni" was all she managed to gasp before falling unconscious. Toni tried to stand but fell headlong on the floor, feeling reality slip away.

Simon had parked his bike and was now making his way on foot towards the filming site, which was in a natural amphitheatre. He took out a pair of binoculars and scanned the site. He could not see Agatha anywhere, but there was Jessica with Rex, just emerging from the catering trailer. He set up the listening device and switched it on. He was hidden behind a thick clump of gorse.

He pointed the listening device towards Jessica and put on the earphones. "It's too hot," Jessica was complaining. "My make-up's beginning to melt." Simon watched and listened as the acting went on.

He saw the scene where Jessica pretended to be bitten by an adder in her thigh and Rex trying to call for help on his mobile and failing.

At last, the day's filming was over. He put his binoculars to his eyes again and saw Jessica and Rex going into a trailer. Now perhaps Jessica just might say something about him. Simon did not stop to wonder about the idiocy of his behaviour or wonder why on earth Jessica should even remember him.

Then he heard Jessica say, "Well, they're both out cold. What do we do with them?"

Rex's voice came loud and clear. "We'll wait until everyone has gone to bed. I'll bring the van round and get the bodies into it. I'll get them into their car and drive it up on the moors. Give the couple of snoops some adder bites and leave them to rot."

"No, don't do that," said Jessica. "The police will be over us like a rash. It'll bring the focus right to us. Take the bodies to the Freemantle woman's garden and dump them there. Have they got enough of the drug in them to knock them out for long enough?"

"Got the stuff at a club last night. Told it was prime."

"I wish we had never started this," said Jessica.

"It was your idea," complained Rex. "You went off your chump when Marston turned you down flat. You said if I didn't help you, you'd get me off the show."

"Oh, stop whining and pour me a drink."

Simon lay behind the bushes, trembling.

Chapter Ten

Simon knew if he phoned the police, the call could be traced to his mobile. He could head off and find a phone box. Could he disguise his voice? Agatha and Toni were drugged. He would need to wait and watch and see if there was some way he could follow Jessica and Rex when they went to finish the job and then call the police. If they were caught in the act outside Mrs. Freemantle's cottage, that would be the best way.

He felt ill when he thought of all Toni's beauty and youth wiped out.

The evening wore on into night. Jessica and Rex had dinner in the catering van and then returned to the trailer. "Set the alarm for two in the morning," ordered Jessica. "I'm bushed."

The hours dragged on. Simon was too frightened and upset to fall asleep.

At two o'clock, he heard the alarm go off,

and Rex say, "I'll get old Rosie's wheelchair." Rosie Buxton was an elderly actress who played the part of a wise old Malvern woman.

Simon's brain worked furiously. Surely there was a gleam of hope. They had talked about a drug and giving them snakebites. But they hadn't said anything about them being dead. He decided to phone the police.

Simon left the listening device under the gorse bushes, and began to run across the moors to where he had parked his motorbike.

Toni groggily came awake. She blinked her eyes. She saw she was in the backseat of Agatha's car and that Rex was driving with Jessica beside him. She quietly leaned towards Agatha, put a hand over her mouth and pushed and prodded her.

Agatha's eyes flew open. Toni put her hand to her lips. Agatha stared at the back of Rex and Jessica's heads.

Simon was standing with the police at a road barrier set up outside Carsely. "You're sure of this?" asked Bill Wong.

"I told you," said Simon. "I suspected them all along and was listening outside their trailer."

Simon had decided to stop at the first

phone box when he got out of the area in Malvern and had phoned the police.

"Aren't you searching the roads from Malvern?" he asked desperately.

"Yes, there's an all-points alert," said Bill. "We'll get them . . . unless you made the whole thing up."

Bill did not approve of Simon. He remembered how Simon had once been chasing Toni, then had gone into the army and got engaged and dumped his bride-to-be at the altar.

Shifty little swine, thought Bill as he gazed anxiously up the road.

"Are we never going to get there?" asked Jessica petulantly.

"I'm keeping to the back roads," said Rex. "Don't want anyone to see the car."

"Where are the snakes?" asked Jessica.

"In the boot. Shut up and let me drive."

Agatha could feel rage building up inside her. If the car slowed enough, she could risk rolling out. But what if Rex had a gun?

She searched in her handbag, looking for something she could use as a weapon, her fingers moving quietly through the contents, frightened any sound would alert Rex. Her fingers closed on a canister of extra-strength lacquer. They were now out on the Fosse Way.

"Hell! Blue lights in the distance," said Rex. "I'll swing off here at Harn." Agatha was hoping he would make a slow turn but he swung the wheel violently, and at the same time, she leaned right forward and sprayed the lacquer into his face.

Rex screamed and let go of the wheel. The car, out of control, plunged into an all-night kebab stand parked on a lay-by. A huge red-hot doner kebab crashed through the front windows of the car and landed on Jessica's lap. A flood of coffee from an urn cascaded into Rex's cut and bleeding face. Agatha and Toni had grabbed on to the back of the front seats and crouched down at the last minute to stop themselves from being thrown forward.

Toni got out and ran into the main road, waving her arms desperately as a police car approached. Then she returned to help Agatha out. They clung on to each other, feeling dizzy. Both had banged their heads.

A police car screeched to a stop and two policemen got out. They went to the car. One called urgently for an ambulance.

A stocky unshaven man erupted onto the scene. "Who gonna pay for this?" he yelled.

"I go out back and then hear this goddamn boom."

"Stand to one side, sir," ordered one of the policemen. "We will take your statement in a moment."

An ambulance from Moreton Hospital came racing up, followed by police cars.

"Are they dead?" asked Agatha.

"Stand back, madam. We'll deal with you directly."

Agatha and Toni watched as the giant kebab was lifted out, and then Jessica. Her face was covered in blood. She moaned faintly as she was lifted onto a stretcher and then into the ambulance. Rex was lifted out next. His body seemed still and lifeless. A paramedic bent down and felt for a pulse and then rose to his feet, shaking his head.

A car arrived with Bill Wong and Inspector Wilkes. Bill went straight to Agatha and Toni.

"What happened? Are you all right? Do you need to go to hospital?"

"We were drugged," said Agatha. "We came to just before they made the turn to Harn. I sprayed Rex's face with hairspray and he crashed."

"Young Simon tipped us off," said Bill. "There are evidently snakes in the boot They planned to dump you in Mrs. Fre mantle's garden and try to put the blame for your deaths on her."

"How did he find out what they meant to do?" asked Toni.

"He was worried about you and was listening outside their caravan."

That listening device, thought Agatha. I'll bet he was using it.

Bill signalled to Alice Peterson. "Take Mrs. Raisin and Miss Gilmour to hospital for blood tests. We'll need evidence they were drugged."

After the blood tests had been taken, Alice tried to get Toni and Agatha to stay in hospital and rest, but both insisted on going to their respective homes.

Agatha wearily let herself into her cottage. She patted her cats and, as she bent down to refill their water bowls, she saw her hands were shaking.

All she wanted to do was to get to bed and wipe out the frightening images of that crash.

She trailed up the stairs and was about to go into her own room when she heard a gentle snore coming from the guest room. harles!

nd where had her fair-weather friend when she had nearly been murdered?

Snoring his dilettante head off, that's what.

She was suddenly consumed with rage. Why couldn't she have a real man around, a man who would look after her and protect her? Well, she was going to start anew. Right now!

Agatha crashed into the spare room, shook the sleeping Charles awake and shouted, "Get out!"

He blinked at her. "What's got your knickers in a twist?"

"Nearly getting murdered, that's what. I don't ever want to see you again."

Agatha stomped off to the kitchen and sat at the kitchen table, shaking.

At last Charles came down the stairs. He went straight to the front door and let himself out. Agatha burst into hysterical tears.

She finally pulled herself together. As she went out of the kitchen to make her way back upstairs, she saw he had left his set of keys to her cottage on a table in the small hall.

She was awakened three hours later by the shrill ringing of her phone. Agatha groaned and glanced at the clock. Nine in the morning. She picked up the receiver.

Alice Peterson's voice came on the lin

"I'm coming to pick you up. You'll need to make a statement."

"I've only had about three hours' sleep," complained Agatha.

"It's got to be done," said Alice. "I'll drive you to your home afterwards and you can go back to bed. Don't speak to the press." Agatha showered and dressed, ignoring the frantic ringing of her doorbell. She assumed the press had arrived. She tried to cover up the dark circles under her eyes with foundation cream, applied powder and then painted a slash of red on her lips.

Wearing a red cashmere trouser suit, she descended the stairs in time to hear Alice shouting through the letterbox that she had arrived. She opened the door. Cameras clicked, reporters shouted questions. Agatha opened her mouth to make a statement, but Alice hissed, "You can't say a damn thing before the court case. Get in the car."

As they headed up out of the village, Agatha asked, "Is she alive?"

"Jessica Fordyce is in intensive care. She is suffering from multiple lacerations and third-degree burns. Rex is dead. He was only doing about forty when he lost control of the car. If he hadn't hit that kebab stand, he'd still be alive."

"So I killed him?"

"Yes."

"Good. What about the producer?"

"Admitted to giving false alibis. Said the show *was* Jessica. Said he thought she couldn't possibly have done it and so saw no harm in lying for her."

"She must be mad," said Agatha.

"From her blood tests, it seems as if she is an amphetamine addict. That can cause psychosis and there seems to be a bit of brain damage. Rex came from a broken home. Had a record of petty theft until he got into modelling and then was discovered. Jessica must have had a hold over him. He knew she had only to hint that she wanted a new leading man and he would have been off the show."

"I think television is an addiction in itself," said Agatha. "There were sad sacks I came across in my public relations days who would pay two thousand pounds a week just to get on television."

As they drove into the outskirts of Mircester, Agatha suddenly saw a man with fair hair, wearing a well-tailored suit. But it wasn't Charles. All of a sudden, she remembered how she had thrown him out. I'm not apologising, she told herself fiercely, trying to fight down the guilty feeling that she had behaved like a madwoman.

Alice drove round to the back of police headquarters to avoid the press. "You should go on holiday," said Alice. "The whole of the world's press will be descending on our village."

Agatha knew in that moment that the villagers would turn against her again. Many had retired for a peaceful life in the country.

Wilkes looked weary as Agatha was ushered into the interviewing room. Some of the other interviewing rooms had been tarted up, but the one she was in was the same old one she knew from before: hard chairs, scarred table, acid green walls. Bill sat beside Wilkes, facing Agatha. He looked every inch the detective. There was no hint in his features that he was a friend.

Bill was actually thinking that Agatha looked well despite her recent experiences. Her brown hair shone in the dim light and her face was well made up.

"What made you suspect them, Mrs. Raisin?" Wilkes began. "Begin at the beginning."

Agatha described how Simon had found out that the producer would do anything to keep Jessica sweet and so that had led her to wondering whether he had lied about her alibis. She then went on to describe how they had been drugged and how she had woken up in time to spray lacquer on Rex's face.

The questioning went on and on, backwards and forwards, until Agatha felt she could scream.

At last Wilkes said, "This whole business hinges on the personality of George Marston. He seems to have been capable of driving women bonkers, and, who knows, maybe even Rex fancied him. What was it about him?"

Agatha had a sudden picture of George in her garden, framed by the flowers. "He was incredibly handsome," she said slowly. "You didn't even think about his false leg. In fact, that gave him more glamour — the wounded hero and all that. He had great charm. I suppose he made every woman feel special. I tell you what, he made me feel feminine and most men have lost that art. Since feminism arrived, men don't feel it necessary to court a woman. I think now he led us all on. I think people falling in love with him was as necessary to him as fresh air. And yet when he was murdered, I couldn't really grieve. It was as if I had walked out of some sort of force field. Can you understand that?"

"Sounds like a lot of psychobabble to me,"

said Wilkes. "Is young Simon using some sort of listening device?"

"No!" said Agatha. "I wouldn't allow it."

"We'll be checking him out. We would like you to be on hand for further questioning."

Toni was next to be interviewed. Agatha offered to wait for her but Toni urged her to go home and get some rest.

Back at the cottage, Agatha dutifully said, "No comment at the moment," to the waiting press. She poured herself a large gin and tonic and went out into the garden. There was already a slight chill in the air, heralding autumn. She sank down into a garden chair and lit a cigarette. Her cats chased each other round the lawn.

And then she heard someone calling, "Agatha." She looked to her right. Her ex-husband's head was appearing above the high cedar wood fence. "We're coming over," he said.

"Who?"

"Mrs. Bloxby's here. We're avoiding the press. Have you got a ladder?"

Agatha brought a ladder from the garden shed and propped it against the fence. Mrs. Bloxby climbed gingerly down while James scrambled over.

"Come and sit down," said Agatha. "I'm so glad to see you. Can I get you something to drink?"

"You stay where you are," said James. "What'll you have, Mrs. Bloxby?"

"Just coffee, please."

When James went into the house, Mrs. Bloxby said, "I heard about it on the radio. I don't think they're releasing that much except to say they have arrested someone, but it's all over the village about the accident at Harn."

"I'll tell you all about it when James comes back," said Agatha. She blew a smoke ring up into the air. "I wonder how I did that," she said. "Can't do it when I try."

James came out with a tray bearing mugs of coffee, sugar, milk and a plate of biscuits.

Agatha told them of her adventures in a weary voice. After having gone over it several times already with Wilkes, she seemed to hear her voice coming back at her.

When she had finished, James said, "I saw Charles arriving yesterday. At least you weren't alone last night."

"Oh, did he?" said Agatha. "He must have left before I got up this morning."

"That blush matches your lipstick," said James. He assumed the blush meant Agatha had slept with Charles, and found himself getting annoyed.

"Are you calling me a liar?" shouted Agatha.

"Yes. You're almost as much a philanderer as George Marston."

"That's not true and that's not fair. You know Charles uses my cottage like a hotel!"

"Please," begged Mrs. Bloxby. "Mrs. Raisin has been through a most terrible ordeal. Don't shout."

James rose to his feet. "I think I'd better leave. If you feel you can get round to telling me the truth, Agatha, let me know."

"Snakes and bastards! What the hell has my private life got to do with you? You're my ex, remember?"

James stalked off and climbed over the fence.

A tear rolled down Agatha's cheek and plopped into her gin.

"What really is the matter?" asked Mrs. Bloxby gently. "Is it all the shock? Maybe you should get counselling."

Agatha wiped the tear away. "It's not that," she said. "It's Charles. I came home after being nearly killed and there he was, snoring peacefully in the spare room. I lost my head. I told him to get out."

"Why?"

"I thought a real man would have looked after me."

"Oh, Mrs. Raisin. How on earth was the poor man to know what you had just been through? And you cannot expect people to suddenly change their characters to suit the moment."

"Anyway, he'll never speak to me again and James has gone off in a huff. The village is crawling with press again and they'll all blame me."

"Perhaps you should take a holiday."

"I can't," wailed Agatha. "The police want me to hang around for more questioning."

Both women fell silent. Slowly Agatha began to feel calmer. It was almost as if the vicar's wife emanated peace and quiet.

At last Mrs. Bloxby said, "Has it occurred to you that Miss Fordyce could be found innocent?"

Agatha stared at her. "That's not possible. She was caught red-handed with the pair of us recovering from drugs in the backseat. How on earth . . ."

"If she knows Rex is dead, she can plead that he manipulated her and terrified her and that he committed the murders."

Agatha took out her phone and managed to get through to Bill Wong. "Does Jessica know that Rex is dead?" she asked. "If she does, she can blame everything on him."

"We've thought of that. She will be available for an interview possibly later today. Everyone has had strict instructions not to discuss the case with her."

When Agatha rang off, she said, "Well, that's all right. She's not to be told."

Jessica felt very weak and terrified that her face might be damaged beyond repair. A young nurse came in to monitor the various tubes attached to Jessica's body.

"What is your name?" asked Jessica faintly.

"Mary Donovan, miss."

"Bring me a mirror, Mary."

"I don't think you should be bothering about that now. Just you get better. To think of the times I've watched you on the telly."

"Tell me. Is Rex dead?"

"Now the police have been after saying no one's to discuss the case with you. Just get some rest."

"Please, Mary. It's not discussing the case. I have to know. Look, I'm innocent and when I get back on television, I'll find a part for you."

"My! Me on the telly."

"Why not?"

There were footsteps in the corridor outside. "Yes, the poor lad is dead," whispered Mary, just as a doctor entered the room.

"Doctor," said Jessica. "Is my lawyer here yet?"

"The police are coming to interview you later today and I believe he will be present then."

Jessica thought furiously. There was a way out of all this. She would pretend to be even weaker than she was to postpone the interview.

The following April, on a blustery windy day, Agatha, Toni and Simon stood outside the Old Bailey under the entrance sign: DEFEND THE CHILDREN OF THE POOR AND PUNISH THE WRONGDOER.

"I need a drink," grumbled Agatha. "The defence made *me* feel like the wrongdoer." The three detectives were feeling emotionally battered after being interrogated by Jessica's defence, Lord Hollinsby.

Simon had been the longest in the witness stand. Lord Hollinsby had dragged up Simon's aborted marriage and ignominious departure from the army on psychiatric grounds. Then a whole day was taken up while the jury were escorted to Jessica's trailer and asked to listen outside while two people talked inside. All said they couldn't hear a thing.

Toni was next. She put up a good show in

the witness box, sticking calmly to her guns as she described the drugging and abduction.

Agatha had been grilled that morning. Before she took the stand, Mrs. Arnold from the village testified to Agatha's passion for George Marston, followed by Joyce Hemingway, who described Agatha Raisin as "hysterical."

Then it was Agatha's turn and she unfortunately lost her temper and called Lord Hollinsby an idiot if he thought Jessica Fordyce was an innocent victim of Rex Dangerfield. She knew she had given a bad impression.

They went over to the Firefly pub and ordered drinks and food. "How Jessica managed to get out on bail is beyond me," said Agatha. "I think she must have had some plastic surgery. She's in the box this afternoon. I don't think the prosecution is doing a very good job. Surely she can't get away with it."

"She might," said Toni. "The charge is murder. She had that top psychiatrist who swears that she was terrified of Rex. If only she didn't have all that money to pay for top defence and famous psychiatrist. I've never believed those people who grumble that there's one law for the rich and one for the poor, but I think I'm seeing that very thing in action."

"Simon," said Agatha. "I'm going to ask you again. Did you use that listening device?"

"Well, I did," said Simon defiantly, "and if I hadn't, you'd both be toast."

"May I remind you that I saved us," snapped Agatha. "You said you'd taken it home in case the police searched the office. Where is it now?"

"I buried it in your garden."

"You what? When?"

"It wasn't long after the arrest. I thought they might search my flat so one time I was visiting you and you were in the house on the phone, I buried it."

"You idiot. All you've done is make it look as if you made the whole thing up."

"Simon was worried about us," said Toni.

"I've never understood why you didn't call the police right away," raged Agatha. "They'd have been caught with two drugged bodies and a lot of explaining to do."

"I wanted them actually caught in the act. I mean, if the police arrived, they could just say you had drunk too much."

"What about her cracked alibis?" asked Toni.

"According to Patrick's police sources,

they still can't place her at any of the murders. When Mrs. Glossop was attacked, they only have her word for it that she was having dinner in Moreton."

"Surely other diners would remember such a celebrity," said Toni.

"Well, there was a time gap when they could have returned to Carsely. I mean, I nearly caught one of them in the act. We'd better get back soon. Patrick's keeping places for us."

When Jessica took the witness box, there was a moment of pure theatre. A shaft of sunlight shone down through a dusty window and illuminated her like a spotlight.

She seemed more beautiful than ever. Her face was cleverly made up: white with shadows under her eyes. Agatha reflected sourly that she had not seen such a clever job of make-up since Princess Diana's famous *Panorama* interview when she said there were three in the marriage.

As the cross-examination began, Agatha realised with a sinking heart that, just because Jessica starred in a soap opera, she had discounted her acting abilities. Jessica was putting on an Oscar performance.

In a halting voice, she described her terror of Rex. Rex had said that if she did not do his bidding, he would not only kill her but her mother as well. He would know the minute she contacted the police.

"Her mother?" whispered Agatha to Patrick.

"Quite mad. In an asylum. Jessica never visits her," mumbled Patrick.

"Shhh!" complained an angry voice behind them.

Jessica's voice broke occasionally. Her hands fluttering in a touching gesture of appeal, she looked at the jury. "Rex was obsessed with George Marston. He said if he couldn't have him, nobody would. He said that George's behaviour, having affairs with old women, was disgusting and that they should all be wiped off the planet."

And then she broke down and cried.

To Agatha's dismay, a woman on the jury began to dab her eyes.

Jessica was asked by the judge whether she would like a recess, but she dried her eyes and said she would go on.

The prosecutor did his best, but ended up looking like some sort of brutal bullying villain.

The court finally rose. "Let's hope the judge's summing up cuts through the crap," said Agatha.

■ ■ ■ ■

They returned the following day. Lord Hollinsby gave an impassioned defence. The prosecutor gave a dry, concise attack. The summing up by the judge was balanced but, in Agatha's opinion, there were too many "on the other hands" in it. She had hoped for an outright condemnation.

The jury retired to consider their verdict.

There was no result on the following day, but they were told the day after that that the jury had returned.

The verdict was not guilty.

A great cheer shook the court.

"Let's get out of here," said Agatha. "I feel sick."

It had been raining, but when Jessica emerged to face the barrage of the world's press, the sun had come out.

"I can only say that I am overcome with gratitude," said Jessica, and then was hustled to a limousine by two bodyguards.

"Not much of a statement," said Toni.

"Means she'd sold her story to the highest bidder," said Agatha cynically. "I feel awful. Let's all go home."

Jessica had sold her cottage in Carsely. As

another summer arrived, the village settled back into its usual Cotswold torpor as if it had never been rent by murder. Joyce Hemingway and Mrs. Freemantle had also sold up and left. George's sister would inherit his cottage and estate after a long legal process, so George's cottage remained empty.

Agatha had seen nothing of Charles. She had tried to call several times but had been told firmly by his man, Gustav, that he was not at home. She had written to him and sent e-mails but there was never any reply. James was abroad and even Roy had turned down the offer of a week-end. Agatha was feeling friendless, despite the comfort of visits from Mrs. Bloxby and Bill Wong.

She had to admit to herself that she really missed Charles. She had not read Jessica's story, which had been published in a Sunday newspaper. Agatha thought that Jessica would always go down in her mind as her one big failure.

She had decided to take a holiday but didn't relish the idea of travelling on her own.

The listening device had been recovered from her garden and placed in a cupboard under the kitchen sink.

One sunny Saturday morning, Bill Wong

called. "What's happened?" asked Agatha, ushering him through to the garden.

"Nothing at all in the way of dramatic crime. But have you heard the news about Charles?"

"What? Is he all right?"

"Oh, yes. It's just that I read about his engagement in the *Times* this morning."

"Not that Petronella creature?"

"No, it's someone called Crystal Stretton, daughter of a Colonel and Mrs. Stretton. Didn't he tell you?"

"No. As a matter of fact I haven't seen him for nearly a year. You see, I was overwrought that night Jessica tried to kill me and I found him in the spare room. I went ape and told him to get out."

"Still, he must have read about your ordeal in the papers."

"He wouldn't get all the facts until the trial report and that would make me look like the man-hunting harpy from hell."

"An apology should do the trick."

"I e-mailed him. I wrote snail mail. I've tried phoning."

"Yes, but did you actually apologise?"

"Not really. I was going to do that face-to-face."

"So you just said something like 'get in touch.' "

"Something like that. He should have *understood*," said Agatha.

"Not unless he's gifted with ESP. There's also news in the paper about Jessica."

"What's she done now? Flipped her lid and killed someone else?"

"No such luck. I'd still like to nab her somehow," said Bill. "She's going to Hollywood next month. Landed a part starring opposite Tom Hanks."

"Isn't she under contract to the soap?"

"Evidently the ratings were plunging and they weren't going to do any more. The fact is that after all that euphoria about her walking free was over, the public began to wonder if she really was innocent."

"And yet Hollywood's not bothered!" exclaimed Agatha.

"She has a good PR, Harry Curry."

"That man never had any morals."

"I'm glad she's leaving the country," said Bill.

"Why?"

"For a time I was worried she might come after you," said Bill. "I was in on her interviews and I could swear she was a hardened psychopath."

"Well, it looks like it's going to stay one of my failures."

"You and the police's," said Bill.

Epilogue

After Bill had left, Agatha mulled over the news about Charles. She felt that once he was married then he would really be lost to her. She eyed the cupboard under the sink where the listening device was kept. Just once, she told herself suddenly. I'll go to his mansion after dark and see if I can learn where he is going to be and maybe waylay him.

The days were growing lighter and it seemed a long time before the sun went down. Dressed in dark clothes, Agatha put the listening device in her car and drove in the direction of Charles's Warwickshire home.

She parked the car under a stand of trees a little short of the drive and set out on foot, hoping she would not come across a game-keeper. She left the drive near the house and cut across the fields so that she could approach the house from the back.

Agatha settled down in a clump of bushes and pointed the machine at the black silhouette of the Victorian mansion.

She could hear the sounds of a late-night news broadcast on a television set. Then the sound of a phone ringing. Gustav's voice came loud and clear. "No, Mrs. Conway. Sir Charles is not at home. He and his fiancée have gone to France." Then Gustav's voice again. "He is travelling by car to Moulins with a view to buying a property in the Auvergne."

Agatha had heard enough. She carefully and silently made her way back to her car, where she sat staring into space, wondering what to do. She hadn't had a holiday in a long time. Perhaps if she went to this Moulins place, she could make her apology.

In the morning, she phoned Doris Simpson and asked her to look after her cats. Then she called Toni and said she would be away for two or three days.

Agatha shoved a few clothes into a suitcase along with a large bag of make-up and then sat down at her computer to map out a journey to Moulins. She looked up the hotels and found Charles had booked into the Hotel Bourbon.

A little voice of common sense in her head kept protesting, "This is madness. You're stalking him." But she told the voice to mind its own business.

She drove to Birmingham Airport and booked herself on to the first flight to Paris. In Paris, she took a taxi to the Gare de Lyon and bought a first-class seat on a train to Moulins.

Only when the train was hurtling through the French countryside did the voice of common sense become increasingly louder.

Well, she told herself, I need a holiday. I don't really need to see him.

She had not booked into the same hotel as Charles. Instead, at Moulins, she took a cab to the Clos de Bourgogne, a pleasant hotel like a French manor house. Before she could weaken, after she had unpacked, she took a cab to the Hotel Bourbon. She did not go into the hotel but walked along the street to a brasserie with outside tables. From there, she could watch the entrance. She felt guilty at not exploring the old town, which had been the seat of the Dukes of Bourbon before the French Revolution. It had a gentle area of prosperous calm with sunlight gilding the old buildings on either side of the narrow streets.

Agatha began to feel weary but relied on a cup of black French coffee and two cigarettes to perk herself up.

And then, quite suddenly, she saw them — Charles and his fiancée. Her heart sank. Crystal Stretton was young and beautiful. She had long blond hair, a perfect face and very good legs revealed by the short filmy summer dress she was wearing. Agatha grabbed a discarded newspaper from a nearby chair and held it up over her face.

She therefore did not see Charles usher the beauty into her car or hear him say, "Thank you for taking the time to show us those houses, but nothing seems to suit. Maybe tomorrow."

Charles went into the hotel to join what he was beginning to think of as the Great Mistake. The real Crystal Stretton was waiting for him in the lounge. She was thin, angular and tall. He reflected that they had not spent much time together before he popped the question or he might have realised just how domineering she was.

Also, as Crystal was very rich, Charles had assumed she would pay for the house in France and their first row had erupted that day when it transpired that Crystal expected him to pay for it.

"I'm just going upstairs for my cigarettes," he said.

"You must stop smoking," said Crystal.

Charles did not reply. He went up to their room. He lit a cigarette and looked out of the window, wondering what to do. As he watched, he saw someone who looked remarkably like Agatha Raisin getting into a cab.

He sat down at his laptop and found the numbers of hotels in Moulins and phoned round until he discovered the one where Agatha was staying.

He was told at the hotel that Mrs. Raisin was having dinner in the garden. He hesitated a moment in the doorway. Candles flickered on the tables. At a table at the edge of the garden sat Agatha Raisin.

She looked sad and tired. He realised in that moment that he had wanted to get away from Agatha, be a family man, lead a "normal" life. But all it had got him was an engagement to a woman who, rich as she was, had turned out to be even meaner than he was himself. Not only that, she was bullying and managing.

He walked into the garden, pulled out a chair opposite Agatha. Charles waved away a hovering waiter.

"Hullo, Aggie."

"Don't call me Aggie."

"Okay, Agatha, what are you doing here?"

"I'm hunting you down to apologise. I did

try so often to contact you. I am very sorry I told you to get out. My nerves were frazzled after the attempt on my life. I suddenly wanted a man to look after me, not to lie snoring in my spare-room bed."

"No one could call your apologies exactly fulsome, Agatha."

"I sometimes want to be an ordinary domesticated woman," sighed Agatha. "Where's your fiancée?"

"Probably wondering where I've gone. Maybe we're not supposed to have so-called normal relationships. I've made a bad mistake."

"She's rich, isn't she?" demanded Agatha.

"But mean with it."

"So are you."

"Not always. Waiter! Champagne!"

Crystal wondered where Charles had gone. When he had rushed out of their hotel, she had been reading a magazine and so had not seen him escape. After searching the whole hotel after she had found their room empty, she ate a solitary dinner. When she went back up to their room, she noticed this time that Charles's computer was switched on, although the screen was dark. She pressed the ENTER button and found herself looking at a Web site of hotels in Moulins.

Beside the laptop was a note: "Clos de Bourgogne."

Crystal ordered a taxi and went to the hotel. To her demands at reception, they said that no Sir Charles Fraith was staying at the hotel.

"Perhaps he is dining here," said Crystal.

"Most of our guests are dining in the garden restaurant," said the receptionist. "I'll show you where it is."

Crystal looked around the garden but there was no sign of Charles. She could hear the English accents of a couple dining at one of the tables.

Crystal took a photo of Charles out of her handbag. "Have you see this man this evening?"

The woman said, "Yes, he went into that cottage over there."

At the edge of the garden was a guest cottage. Crystal strode towards it.

"Oh, Lord," said the woman's husband. "You should have told her he went in there with that woman."

Crystal did not knock. She simply turned the handle and walked in. There was a small hall separating the bathroom from the bedroom and, just coming out of the bathroom, was Charles. He was stark naked.

"What are you doing here?" raged Crystal.

"And cover yourself up. You're indecent!"

In the bedroom, Agatha, who had packed to leave in the morning, slid her suitcase under the bed and then followed it herself.

"I wanted to get away from you," said Charles.

"Who is she? You're not registered here."

Crystal threw open the bedroom door and stared at the seemingly empty room.

"I booked it under another name," said Charles. "You're always yakking at me and I wanted a bit of peace and quiet."

"To think I threw over Brian Fairweather for you," shouted Crystal.

"Then I suggest you pick him up again."

"I never want to see you again," said Crystal, her face mottled with rage. "I'll take a cab to Lyon in the morning and get on the first plane home. Our engagement is over."

After he made sure she had really gone, Charles said, "You can come out now, Agatha."

Agatha crawled out from under the bed.

"Now, where were we?" said Charles.

At one point during the night, Agatha heard him complain, "Damn, I should have asked for my ring back."

"Cheapskate," murmured Agatha, and fell into a heavy sleep.

Two days later, Bill Wong phoned Toni. "Do you know where Agatha is?" he asked. "I called at her home but her cleaner said she was abroad."

"I got a call," said Toni. "She's due back tomorrow. Anything urgent?"

"It's just I feel uneasy about Jessica. I'm always afraid she might try something. She's due to leave for the States next week and I'll be glad when she's out of the country."

The nurse, Mary Donovan, was sitting on a bench outside the hospital, enjoying a cigarette, when a car drove up and stopped opposite her. The windows were very dark — surely illegally dark.

The driver's window slid down. With a gasp, Mary recognised Jessica Fordyce. "Hop in, Mary," said Jessica, and quickly slid the window closed again.

Mary scurried around to the passenger side and got in. "I thought you had forgotten about me," she said.

"As if I would. I'm off to the States, but when the film is over, I'll be returning to do another series, and there will be a part for you. Now, you're not to tell anyone."

"I swear I won't."

"I just want you to do one little thing for me. Here is a photograph of a cat. I want you to go right away to the Agatha Raisin Detective Agency and say it is your lost cat. Ask for Agatha Raisin personally. They will tell you she is out of the country. I phoned today and found that out. Find out when she is due back and call me. Here is a note of my mobile number. And here is a hundred pounds for your trouble."

"But why . . . ?"

"Do you trust me?"

"Oh, yes."

"Then don't ask questions."

Half an hour later, Toni surveyed the new client. When Mary demanded that Agatha alone should deal with her missing cat, Toni said, "That is not possible. Mrs. Raisin is abroad."

"When will she be back?"

"Not until tomorrow. But we are perfectly capable of dealing with your missing cat in her absence."

Toni noticed that the new client's hands were trembling and that her face was covered in a thin film of sweat. Toni turned to Phil, who was fiddling with a camera lens.

"Phil, take a photo of Miss Donovan for

our files."

"No!" shrieked Mary, heading for the door. "I've changed my mind."

"You've left your handbag," called Toni.

Mary swung round and Phil snapped a photo of her. It was then that Mary realised she had her handbag over her arm. She scampered down the stairs and out into the street. She was sure that man hadn't had time to get a picture of her. She wouldn't tell Jessica. Just give her the news about Agatha Raisin's return.

Charles and Agatha arrived back the following afternoon. Agatha suddenly felt awkward. "Coming in?" she asked.

"No, I'm tired. That side trip to Birmingham Airport to pick up your car was a killer. Got to get home. Things to do. People to see." He glanced at her downcast face. "Maybe a coffee to wake me up."

"We'll have it in the garden," said Agatha. "It's a real Indian summer."

In the kitchen, she filled up the coffee percolator from the water filter jug on the counter.

When she carried the tray out into the garden, Charles was half asleep. He sat up. "Just what I need."

Agatha poured black coffee for both of them.

The day had that lazy golden sunshine of autumn. They sat peacefully drinking coffee, Agatha, for once, not feeling she had to demand anything of him.

"I was wondering," began Charles. "Wait a minute. I . . ." He slumped forward over the table.

Agatha began to feel her senses swimming. "Charles," she croaked. "The coffee . . ." And then she, too, collapsed.

Dressed as a boy, Jessica nimbly scaled the cedar wood fence and dropped down into the garden. She was wearing a baseball cap pulled down over her eyes. She had shoved fliers for a charity through several doors in the village. No one really noticed what they thought was a boy delivering leaflets. It had worked before and it would work again. It was bad luck the trick with the Frasers hadn't worked. Rex had gone to them to buy cannabis. They didn't answer the door, so he had gone round to the garden and found a mess of rocks on the lawn and a hole already dug. He had kept a watch from the adjoining field and had seen them put a metal box in the hole and then begin to construct a rockery over it.

She felt secure. She had checked that the neighbour, James Lacey, was away. No one to disturb her. "Here comes your revenge, Rex," she said.

Jessica planned to make it look like a burglary. It had all gone so well. The day before, she had waited until the cleaner had gone into the cottage and listened until she heard her move upstairs. She had let herself in and poured Rohypnol into the water jug.

But first, to finish this precious pair off. She went into the kitchen and rummaged in the cupboard until she found a hammer.

She was just turning to go back into the garden when she was seized from behind. She screamed and dropped the hammer. Her hands were forced behind her back and she was handcuffed.

Bill Wong shouted, "Let them in, Toni," and suddenly the cottage was full of police.

Jessica shouted and raved as she was carried bodily outside.

"If Agatha and Charles are dead," said Toni, "I'll never forgive you."

Agatha awoke eight hours later, puzzled to find herself in a hospital bed. Her mouth was dry. She could not remember anything. She turned in her bed and found Charles in a bed next to her.

Agatha pressed a bell beside her bed. A nurse came in, followed by Bill Wong and Alice Peterson.

"Water," demanded Agatha. "What am I doing here?"

"Maybe it should wait until you're fully recovered."

Agatha took a gulp of water from the glass the nurse was holding out to her. "No, I want to know now. What on earth happened? Why is Charles here as well?"

Bill pulled a chair up to the bed. "A woman, later identified as Mary Donovan from this hospital, called on the agency with some story about a lost cat and asking when you would be back. Toni got suspicious because Donovan was so nervous. She got Phil to take a photo and e-mailed it to me. I recognised it as being one of the nurses who had looked after Jessica.

"So I got a set of keys from your cleaner and let myself in, along with Toni, and had a squad of police waiting concealed at the end of the lane. I looked down into the garden from the bedroom window and saw you and Charles slumped over the garden table. Then I knew Jessica had managed to put something in the coffee or the water.

"I saw her arrive, dressed as a boy, good disguise, you'd never believe it was her, and saw her go into the house. I crept down the stairs and saw her take a hammer out of one of the cupboards. That's when I arrested her. It seems possible that she put Rohypnol into the water jug."

"Wait a minute," said Agatha. "Let me get this straight. You looked down from the bedroom window and saw me and Charles passed out. We could have been given poison. Why didn't you rush us off to hospital?"

"Inspector Wilkes said if we did not catch her in the act, then we would not have a case. I mean," he pleaded, "look at it this way, if you were dead, you were dead. Right? And if she had drugged you, which seems to have been her modus operandi, then she was bound to turn up to finish you off. Don't glare at me, Agatha. We got her at last."

"No, I damn well don't see it that way," said Agatha. "If she had poisoned us and you had been quick off the mark, there might have been time to get our stomachs pumped out."

"We had to take a risk," said Bill.

"You took a risk with our lives."

"You probably don't feel up to making a statement now . . ."

"No, I don't," said Agatha. "Furthermore,

I can't remember a thing. That's Charles waking up. See what he thinks of your story."

Agatha lay back, drifting in and out of sleep as Bill told the story again. She came fully awake at Charles's cry of "What right bastards you are!"

"It was such a long shot," pleaded Bill. "She might not have turned up at all."

"Just get the hell out of here and give us some peace," said Charles.

"We'll be back later when you are feeling yourself again."

"I don't go in for masturbation," said Charles.

A few minutes after Bill and Alice had left, Toni and Simon came in bearing fruit and chocolates.

"I'd like to tell you what happened," said Agatha, "but I can't remember a thing. What about you, Charles?"

"The same."

"Any more news?" asked Agatha.

"Patrick got it from his contacts. There's a fear she might not stand trial. She was all right until they told her that the ancient double jeopardy rule didn't apply anymore and charged her with the murders. They say that was when she went absolutely bonkers."

"I didn't know double jeopardy didn't apply anymore," said Charles.

"There was this chap, Billy Dunlop," said Simon, "who was charged in nineteen-eighty-nine with the murder of twenty-two-year-old Julie Hogg. Julie's mother, Mrs. Ming, ran a fifteen-year campaign to change the double jeopardy rule and finally succeeded. In two thousand and six, Dunlop was charged with the murder again and found guilty."

"It's the cunning of it all!" exclaimed Agatha. "The attempt to frame the Frasers. The viciousness of George's murder. The woman is a monster. She cannot possibly get off this time."

"But she may not stand trial," said Toni.

"I still cannot understand why Bill just lurked around, not trying to see whether Charles and I were still alive."

"He wanted to catch her in the act. If he had called for an ambulance, then Jessica would have cleared off and she would have tried again."

"I want to go home," said Agatha. "Call for the doctor, Toni, and let's see how quickly I can get out of here."

A week later, Patrick burst into the office with the news that Jessica had hanged herself in her cell. Remand prisoners were allowed to wear their own clothes and Jessica had been wearing a thin muslin blouse. She had torn the blouse into strips to make a noose and had hanged herself from the bars of her cell. She had left a note to say that she was "joining dear Rex, the love of my life."

"Bollocks!" said Agatha, exasperated. "The press will have a field day. The fact that Rex was gay will be hidden and she'll turn out to be some sort of tragic heroine."

"Do they have to tell the press about that note?" asked Toni.

"Bound to," said Agatha gloomily. "They'll be such an enquiry."

Agatha's prediction turned out to be true. Fans were even suggesting that there should be a memorial to her in Hyde Park, just like the one to Princess Diana. It was firmly believed by the unbalanced minds in Britain that poor Jessica had being hounded to her death by the police and the Agatha Raisin Detective Agency.

Only when the full report of Jessica's part in the murders came out did the hate mail stop arriving at the agency and the story die in the newspapers.

Agatha still had miserable nights, plagued

by nightmares. Added to that, Charles seemed to have disappeared again. It was all very well to be modern and claim that casual sex was healthy exercise, but Agatha wondered why she fretted so much and felt like a discarded slut.

But two months after Jessica's suicide, Charles phoned, his voice sounding unusually diffident. "I've got two tickets for *Macbeth* at the Royal Shakespeare Company," he said. "Feeling like coming?"

And Agatha, who felt like berating him and screaming at him that he had no right to use her and walk out of her life, said, "I haven't seen the new theatre at Stratford. When are we going?"

"Tonight, if you're free."

"Okay."

"I'll pick you up at six this evening. We'll have a drink in the bar first."

Agatha called on Mrs. Bloxby. "Charles has asked me out on a date," she said.

Mrs. Bloxby looked puzzled. "But you have been lots of places together before."

"But this is a real date! The theatre! I mean it's only been foreign stuff before and meals — but he is taking me out!"

Mrs. Bloxby felt her heart sink. If Agatha fell in love with Charles it would be a disaster. She would expect nothing less than marriage and that would mean a lifestyle as lady of the manor that Mrs. Bloxby felt sure Agatha would find crippling.

"Perhaps he won the tickets in a raffle and no one else was available to go with him," said the vicar's wife.

"What a catty thing to say," said Agatha huffily. "I'm off!"

But deep down, Agatha felt, as she dressed for the evening, that there had been something that might just be true in Mrs. Bloxby's comment.

Charles arrived, casually dressed in jacket and trousers and open-necked shirt. Agatha was in the full glory of a little black dress, a ruby necklace, and scarlet high heels.

"You're very grand," said Charles. "Won't you feel cold?"

"I've got a stole," said Agatha. "Should I change?"

"No, you're fine. It's just that people don't dress up anymore."

Charles parked the car in Stratford-Upon-Avon and they approached the new theatre on foot. "Is that it?" exclaimed Agatha. "It looks like a fire tower, and all that redbrick!"

They walked into the stalls bar, a bleak

place in grey and black. It did not look like a theatre bar, but like part of some warehouse that had been hurriedly transformed for the evening.

"At least I know the play," said Agatha.

"Well, let's hope they're faithful to it," said Charles. "How are you anyway? Got over all the frights?"

"I still get a few nightmares," said Agatha. "In fact," she said, casting him a sideways look out of her bearlike eyes, "I've sometimes thought of chucking the whole thing up and settling down."

"Settling down as what?" asked Charles.

As your wife, would have been the honest reply. "Oh, I don't know," said Agatha warily. "My shares are doing well, despite the recession. I may give up work. I'm quite domesticated, really."

"If nuking every meal in the microwave is your idea of domesticity — sure."

The bell for the start of the performance rang and they went into two good seats in the stalls.

There were several shocks for Agatha. The actor playing Macbeth was small and balding. Banquo, on the other hand, was a tall, powerful, black man with dreadlocks. There were no witches. The witches had been cancelled and replaced with three child actors with piping voices. Sometimes it was hard to hear the actors because of it being a theatre in the round. Instead of talking out to the audience as they would have done in a more conventional theatre, the actors spoke to one another, often with their backs to where Agatha and Charles were seated. The interval came as a relief.

Or that was until Charles introduced Agatha to two friends of his, Barry and Mary Tring.

"Enjoying it?" boomed Barry, a tall man with a florid face.

"Not much," said Charles.

"You should have seen *The Merchant of Venice*," said Barry. "Set in Las Vegas and opened with an Elvis Presley impersonator, singing 'Viva Las Vegas.' "

"Well, it's never about Shakespeare," said Charles, "but all about the producer. I'm sorry for the American tourists. They like their Shakespeare straight."

"Just be glad you won those tickets at the cricket club do," said Barry.

Agatha suddenly wanted to go home. But the bell was ringing, and back they went to endure the rest of the play. At one point the stage seemed to be messy with small children. The ghosts of Macduff's children scurried about with the three elves who had replaced the witches.

At last it was over. Some brave man behind Agatha shouted "Boo!" very loudly but everyone else clapped politely.

On the road home, Charles kept up a polite chatter about the play.

Outside Agatha's cottage, she surprised him by getting out of the car and saying briefly, "See you." No invitation to come in for a drink.

Agatha slammed the door and stormed into her kitchen. He hadn't even suggested taking her for dinner. She kicked off her shoes and put a curry in the microwave.

"I'm a silly old slut," she said to her cats. "Men! I've given them up."

But after she had eaten and had downed two large glasses of wine, she began to relax.

The world was full of men. Out there, surely, was some man who would cherish her.

Until then, there were cases to solve.

Damn Charles!

ABOUT THE AUTHOR

M. C. Beaton, the British guest of honor at Bouchercon 2006, has been hailed as the "Queen of Crime" (*The Globe and Mail*). She is the author of twenty-two previous Agatha Raisin novels, whose fans range from the actress Elizabeth Hurley to the Archbishop of Canterbury. Born in Scotland, she now divides her time between Paris and the English Cotswolds.

The employees of Thorndike Press hope you have enjoyed this Large Print book. All our Thorndike, Wheeler, and Kennebec Large Print titles are designed for easy reading, and all our books are made to last. Other Thorndike Press Large Print books are available at your library, through selected bookstores, or directly from us.

For information about titles, please call:
(800) 223-1244

or visit our Web site at:
http://gale.cengage.com/thorndike

To share your comments, please write:
Publisher
Thorndike Press
10 Water St., Suite 310
Waterville, ME 04901